Curious Affairs

Curious Affairs

MARY JANE MYERS

PAUL DRY BOOKS
Philadelphia 2018

First Paul Dry Books Edition, 2018

Paul Dry Books, Inc.
Philadelphia, Pennsylvania
www.pauldrybooks.com

Copyright © 2018 Mary Jane Myers

A version of "Galileo's Finger" first appeared in *PoemMemoirStory* (Number 12, 2013). Used by permission.

Printed in the United States of America

Print ISBN 978-1-58988-150-1

For Eva Brann
and Kerry Madden-Lunsford

with gratitude

*Warm thanks to my editor
Julia Sippel
for her remarkable intelligence
and understanding*

Contents

The Maui Stone   1

Money Dragons   30

Galileo's Finger   48

The Beautiful Lady   61

Sappho Resurgent   66

Beef Medallions   89

A Day at Versailles   94

Recovery   104

The Curious Affair of Helen and Franz   112

GaGa's Piano   138

The Seraphita Sonata   159

The Carpaccio Dog   177

The Miracle of the Shellflowers   183

Curious Affairs

The Maui Stone

As a teenager, Diane Hatcher had been a good Catholic girl. In college she stopped going to Mass except at Christmas and Easter, and in the last two decades, had reflexively hidden any overt sign of religiosity. "Oh, I'm not religious, but of course I'm spiritual, you can pray anywhere"—how many times had she repeated that secular platitude at posh parties, angling for the approval of the glitterati. A month before her forty-third birthday, she welcomed in the New Year, 1995, at a beach house in Malibu. Gliding into a crowded room in a pink satin dress that emphasized her size six figure, she scanned her surroundings. A tall and reed slender man flashed a white-veneered smile. A barbered twenty-day beard framed his face, and gold chains gleamed in the v-neck of his purple silk shirt.

"Hello, I'm Mark."

"Diane. This is a wonderful evening, isn't it?"

"I ne'er saw true beauty till this night."

Smirking she said, "That particular romance didn't end very well."

He laughed. "Ah, but teenagers are hopelessly stupid. You, I can tell, are bright as well as lovely."

How ridiculous, thought Diane, even as she enjoyed the slightly sleazy seduction. The room was dimly lit, crowded and noisy. Gloria, an acquaintance from work, was a friend-of-friends of the hosts, and had talked Diane into coming. Gloria was five years older, twice divorced and never a mother (three abortions, she confided, alarming Diane with this offhand sharing). Their avowed purpose at this party was a manhunt, their tactical agreement to separate at the front door.

Gloria had agreed to drive, and picked up Diane at her Santa Monica apartment south of Pico, ten blocks from the ocean. Gloria floored the accelerator of the red Miata, and sped madly north on PCH. Diane scooched down in her seat, looking not at the road, but at the dashboard. She owned a Ford Taurus—safe and boring—and was a little-old-lady driver, used to being honked at by the arrogant owners of Mercedes and Lexus sedans. At least drunk driving wouldn't be a problem, as Gloria was a "friend of Bill," with three years sobriety. Diane had forever been a teetotaler.

They left the party together at one in the morning. Diane smelled alcohol on Gloria's breath, but did not say anything. All the way back, the two prattled about the possibilities. Gloria had given her phone number to three men, one of whom was Mark—the only man to whom Diane had given hers. Diane was relieved when Gloria pulled the Miata up to the curb in front of Diane's apartment.

At eight o'clock the next morning the telephone rang, Mark's brassy voice on the line. By the end of their ten-minute conversation, Diane had already surrendered.

❄

Mark was forty-seven, a Jungian therapist whose Century City practice was booked solid with anorexic actresses and the neurotic wives of movie producers. An acrimonious five-year marriage in his twenties had soured him on matrimony. Weekends they spent together at his bachelor digs in the Marina. Every weeknight at eight o'clock he telephoned. The talk was smutty, but not quite telephone sex. She imagined him sprawled on the dark green Morocco leather sofa, dressed in the maroon paisley silk bathrobe she had given him. He held the television remote control in one hand, flipping channels every ten seconds, the mute button set, while he cradled the phone in his other hand. A large photograph of three men was displayed in an acrylic stand on the coffee table. In the middle stood the Dalai Lama in an orange robe, his face as beatific as a Forli angel. On the monk's right a grinning Mark posed, his characteristic silk shirt open, showing off the dark curls of his chest hair, gold glinting at his neck. On the other side, a somber Richard Gere stared at the camera. She thrilled to this image of Mark, but a matriarchal inner voice admonished her not to waver, not to allow it. What "it" was, she could not say exactly—his mastery over that simpering girlish element that floated in her psyche.

After five months of ecstatic coupling, he sat Diane down for a lecture, handing her a to-do list to correct bad habits. Bieler's broth and raw vegetables would purge her body of poisons. She should attend a past-life regression group to erase her old Roman Catholic negative tapes. Daily meditation was crucial to calm her chaotic energy that was disturbing his hard-won serenity. A trip together to Maui was on the agenda, a test of her willingness to change.

A child of the midwestern prairie, Diane had always loathed islands, especially those of the paradise variety. They resembled cages, their inhabitants unable to escape, and running endlessly in one place, like pet hamsters on toy Ferris wheels. Her light complexion was allergic to tropical sun. She was wary of scraping herself on coral and unnerved by translucent jellyfish that floated in the surf.

"It's beautiful there. The sea, the breezes, the sun. It's close to nature, close to Spirit," Mark said.

Mark's concepts fascinated Diane, but their heretical oddity alarmed her. This "Spirit" he constantly invoked seemed to have little to do with her idea of the Christian Holy Spirit, a sweet white dove that fluttered overhead and radiated featherweight grace to any soul who prayed. She thought Mark's Spirit sounded like a black broody hen squatting intrusively over the entire universe, with no boundary between its heavy belly and the soul-eggs squashed beneath it.

The threat was implicit. Accompany him to Maui, or else.

His travel agent booked a seven-night package, a bargain consolidator rate for a two-bedroom condominium with ocean views, the quintessential Biblical span in which to seal their perfect union in a Maui Garden of Eden. Diane suggested going Dutch, and Mark didn't object. She flinched as she wrote the check, a huge dent in the emergency fund she had cobbled together from her modest salary as an administrative assistant at a national accounting firm in a fifty-story downtown high-rise.

In late June, a week before departure, she telephoned her childhood friend Angela to talk about the travel plans. The two women seldom got together, but they touched base every few months. They had played wild horses in the empty lots choked with weeds, behind the new suburban tract houses that had cropped up near their Glenvale, Illinois subdivision. In the springtime tadpoles hatched in the mud puddles, and in winter the girls skated on the ice patches that dotted the fields. Through serendipitous twists and turns, Angela lived less than a mile from Diane. She was a successful academic, a tenured professor at Loyola Marymount, an expert in nineteenth-century British literature, whose husband, also a professor, had been killed in an automobile accident seven years earlier. Diane and Angela had taken separate paths in life. But there was always the shorthand of those wild horses.

Diane gushed her delight, painting Maui in gaudy colors like a Gauguin Tahitian landscape. But her voice had an undercurrent of doubt, perhaps even a smidgen of panic.

"I thought you didn't like the tropics."

"I don't normally, but this is different. With Mark, I'll learn so much. He's been a bunch of times, and knows a lot of people, he's a superstar in the New Age world."

There was a silence on the line. Then Angela said, "I'm not being critical, but are you sure this guy's right for you? I only met him briefly that one time, and I didn't say anything, but now I'll tell you straight out—he doesn't seem like a nice man."

Diane said, "I'll be careful. I can't back out now. Anyway, I want to make it work. It's exciting, he's so much more interesting than all the other guys I've dated." She promised to send Angela a postcard.

❄

At the Maui airport they picked up a bright blue Neon rental car. Mark commandeered the wheel, and sped them twenty miles to the condominium complex, a hodgepodge of thin-walled concrete and stucco structures resembling gigantic half-assembled Legos. It was late afternoon, near twilight. There was no elevator, so they each lugged suitcases up a flight of concrete stairs to their unit. A violet expanse of ocean was barely visible from a sliding glass door that led to a rough concrete patio fenced with a flimsy stainless steel railing. Mark was insistent that they walk immediately to the ocean. Diane felt uneasy. Her strict father had trained her to first unpack and organize her belongings when arriving at any new place. She said nothing. Already she was counting the days until their return flight.

They walked through the complex, past scraggly palm trees drooping in concrete planters, out a rusty wrought iron gate, and across the highway to a narrow strip of pebbly beach. Mark pointed to the sunset as if it were his own creation.

Diane agreed. "It's nice." She did not say that the sky's dull russet color lacked the flair of Turner's palette of coquelicot and Indian yellow. It had been expensive to come all this way, and the reality of this storied island should not only match, but indeed should surpass the effects of mere daubed pigments, even those achieved by genius painters. Apparently her money was wasted. She wanted to turn around and go home. They ate dinner at a vegetarian restaurant in a strip mall a half-mile away, and split the check. Sleep was sound that first evening, as the journey had tired them out.

The next day they lazed about, Diane absorbed in *Bleak House*, as she was on a Dickens kick. She was irritated by a character who frequently referred to himself in the third person when he spoke: "The butterflies are free. Mankind will surely not deny to Harold Skimpole what it concedes to the butterflies." Somehow, he reminded her of Mark. She pushed down this thought. Ridiculous to compare an exaggerated Victorian villain to the real life Mark, who rode herd on his pager and talked nonstop on the condo telephone with mysterious contacts who shared his passion for holistic knowledge.

Mark's food discipline was strict: all organics. In the early morning he had sent her out to an organic food market three miles away. His precise list included two dozen eggs and enough sprouted grain bread and fruit to make breakfasts the entire week, and also lunch food for a day trip he was planning for tomorrow. The cost of all this upset her, almost twice that of the Vons where she shopped in Los Angeles, more expensive even than the upscale Gelson's she avoided. At his request she also purchased, for an exorbitant price at a nearby convenience store, a small Coleman cooler and blue ice, items which they would have to leave behind when they returned home. She had charged a total of $220 on her Visa, as he said it would be too complicated to use two credit cards.

He didn't mention reimbursing her, and she was afraid to bring it up because she feared the label of a nitpicky cheapskate, and that he would point out her "money issues." She could only hope he voluntarily would square the account later, though she suspected he would conveniently forget. At sunset, they walked on the beach, ate at the vegetarian restaurant, and split the check—already "our" place, said Mark, though Diane secretly longed for a green salad tossed with white meat chicken chunks, and had made a mental note of both a Baskin Robbins and a hamburger place, neighbor tenants in the strip mall.

On the third day, in midmorning, they departed on an excursion, the destination a surprise. Mark stated that one other person would be joining them. To add a little sex appeal, Diane donned a skimpy tee and a beribboned straw sunhat, but the rest of her outfit was practical, loose-fitting hiking capris and running shoes. Mark wore a pineapple-pattern Hawaiian silk shirt, slim black jeans, and Doc Martens boots, gold shimmering around his neck and wrists. They threw light coats in the back seat, Diane a nylon windbreaker, Mark an Italian leather jacket. Diane had made and packed into the cooler a picnic lunch, three turkey breast sandwiches on a sprouted grain flourless bread, a stash of raw carrots and celery, six apples and the same number of energy bars, three raw peanut-butter coconut cookies, and also six bottles of Geyser spring water and unfiltered pomegranate juice.

Mark drove the Neon five miles inland, to a trailer parked in the red clay earth next to a sugar cane field. Cicadas trilled an earsplitting plainsong. A stout native Hawaiian woman dressed in a lime green cotton overshirt and black shorts opened the trailer door. Inside, a middle aged man and two long-haired tattooed adolescent boys hunkered in a dark room paneled in fake wood, staring at the flicker of the television, where Vanna White was spinning the Wheel of Fortune.

The woman grinned with white, gapped teeth, and encased first Mark and then Diane in mama-bear hugs. Her multisyllabic native name beginning in K and ending in A was unintelligible to an American ear, but she called herself Kate for the benefit of tourists.

Mark turned to Diane. "Kate is a priestess in the old religion. She's connected to Spirit. She's our guide today."

Okay, thought Diane, this should be a memorable adventure. Mark's labyrinthine network astonished and intrigued her. The trio set out, Mark at the wheel, Diane paging through her Fodor's guidebook in the front seat, Kate sprawled over half the back seat. The radio was off, and the three were silent, taking in the primordial wildscape, remarking on the occasional flash of flocks of red or yellow birds. Once they spotted a huge tubular brown rodent.

"Ah, a mongoose," Kate said.

"Rikki Tikki Tavi," Diane said, and when there was no response, "You know, that brave mongoose character in Kipling, he's a pet, and he saves his human family from cobras."

Mark said, "Those old imperialist tapes, I would never let a child anywhere near Kipling."

After a half hour, Kate motioned toward an unmarked paved road that wound up a hillside. At the summit was a field of black pumice rubble. Each stone was about one foot in diameter, pockmarked with white and orange lichen. Kate pointed out square structures three feet high constructed from the stones. It was here, on these altars, she intoned, that healing rituals were performed by the ancestors.

Diane walked up to an altar, boosted her body up, and sat on the top. On one side, the ocean waters sparkled turquoise and lapis blue. On the other side, in the far distance, stood a range of emerald mountains. Rainforest clouds covered their peaks. In the near view, between two cement buildings, was a brown clay lot. A high chain link fence enclosed the lot, behind which two mastiffs paced back and forth. Diane shuddered. She sensed what Kate left unsaid, that captive slaves had been sacrificed here, that their angry spirits hovered over the site.

Diane started back toward the car. Kate walked by her side and unexpectedly put an arm around her shoulders. Startled, Diane drew back.

Kate said, "Don't be scared, everything's OK, I won't let anything bad happen."

Diane said, "I'm not scared, I'm just a little jumpy. Must be jet lag."

Mark had been walking a little ahead, and turned around frowning. "It's not jet lag, there's not enough of a time difference."

"That's true," said Diane. "I don't know why, but I'm a little off-balance. Anyway, Kate, thank you for showing us around. This scenery is spectacular, like a lost kingdom in a fairy tale."

They continued for two hours on the road that meandered by the coast, snacking on energy bars, stopping several times at basalt outcroppings on beaches of pebbly sand. All the sites were unexcavated, not described in the guidebook.

"Why aren't these places documented?" Diane finally asked, exasperated. Kate was vague. These were holy places, sacred to the gods and never disclosed to outsiders.

Mark commented that the silly guidebooks written by westerners were all wrong. "They're trapped inside their own heads, and they simply don't get it," he said. Whenever he invoked the "it" Diane never dared ask him to explain exactly what he meant. His tone somehow replicated her father's: it's my way, or some treacherous highway.

In mid-afternoon, they reached a volcanic formation next to the ocean. Two hundred years ago, an earth-god had extruded hot molten lava, which cooled and molded into an undulating black and gray moonscape. The road crossed over a solid black lava bed. To their left, the land-side, lay a gigantic black lava field, to their right, toward the ocean, the lava disappeared beneath breaking waves. Wind and water had created a pebbly beach that stretched in both directions along the surf.

Mark parked the Neon on the lava bed. The air was sweltering, even with the ocean breeze, the black stone absorbing the heat from a fierce sun in a cloudless sky. Kate opened the trunk and removed two papayas wrapped in broad flat leaves. She chanted a tuneless abracadabra, and gave one to each of them. Her instructions were to lay the papayas on the ground as offerings, after first whispering prayers. Mark grabbed his papaya, and sprinted away, toward the ocean.

What a farce, Diane thought. She picked up the papaya to play out her assigned role. Turning away from the ocean, she crossed the road, and hopping from slab to slab of the black lava for several hundred feet, she found a crevice, sat down, and placing the papaya inside, raised her palms in blessing.

A slight prickle of fear jabbed her. What if these local

spirits, whoever they were, didn't like her flippant attitude? Or worse yet, what if she angered her own Catholic God for playing around with other silly little gods?

She made a half-hearted attempt to appease the divine. "Please, dear God, forgive me. I know it looks like I'm worshipping false idols. I'm only trying to please Mark, and I must be polite to Kate, and yes, I'm curious about Kate's religion, but in an academic sense, to educate myself, to expand my narrow horizons."

She rose to walk back to the road. Suddenly, she heard a deafening noise, a savage buzz all around her, could it be a swarm of Africanized killer bees? Confused, she stared straight up into the sun drenched sky. Perhaps some Japanese developer had built a power transmission tower near this remote spot, and planned to build a luxury resort. But no electrical wires were visible overhead. And now, she was panicking. The awe of her Catholic childhood gripped her full force. As a schoolgirl, she had genuflected with reverence in front of the Host enshrined on the altar. The gloom of the Gothic nave heightened her dread as she waited in the confessional line on Saturday afternoons.

She ran pell-mell toward the Neon, scrambling over the black basalt. Her sunhat blew off, but she didn't stop to retrieve it. Out of breath and dizzy, her heart pounding, she staggered as if intoxicated, and crumpled against the car door, blubbering incoherent half-sentences, holding her ears.

"The sound . . . are they bees? I can't see any bees."

Kate sat on the trunk of the car, surveying the rocky landscape. She smiled, heaved her solid body off the car, and enfolded the younger woman in her arms. The sound stopped.

Diane whimpered as if she were a three year old being comforted by her mother after falling off a jungle gym.

Kate helped Diane sit on the ground, out of the direct sunlight, in the shadow cast by the Neon. Kate waited in silence. After ten minutes, Diane got up, woozy and wobbly, and spied the sunhat, a bright pink splash on the black lava. Never mind. Let it be left behind. She must stay on the ocean side of the road, and avoid that hot wilderness moon zone on the far side.

Mark had disappeared. The two women spotted him on the beach a hundred yards away. He waved, and they followed him, wading into the surf. The waves crashed, and eddies of salt water whirled among the rocks, the dense foam bubbling white against the black boulders. Countless smooth dark-gray pebbles lay on the beach. Diane picked up one of the stones, a four-inch ellipsis, its bland surface flecked with mica. She meant to toss it into the sea, but on a whim she slipped it into her pocket. A souvenir, a Maui stone that she could save among her mementos.

"Let's eat," Mark suggested when they returned to the Neon.

Diane brought out the cooler, and passed out sandwiches to her companions. She wasn't hungry, so she took tiny bites from a fragment of a cookie. Its gummy texture and moldy smell made her queasy. She swallowed three ibuprofens, turning away so Mark wouldn't see.

On the return ride, Kate leaned forward from the back seat, and she and Mark chatted about the acquaintances they had in common, ancient-religion locals and New Age transplants living upcountry in the highlands. Diane slumped immobile in the front seat, the conversation ebbing and flowing, faraway, as if a wall separated her from them. Her head throbbed. Once she turned to look at Kate, who smiled and patted her arm.

"You OK?" Kate asked.

Diane said, "My head is splitting, must be the sun. Sorry to be so grumpy."

Mark kept his eyes on the road, but his sharp retort hurtled directly at Diane. "Who ever heard of the life-giving Maui sun harming anyone?"

Kate said, "It's not uncommon for fair-skinned foreigners to be overcome by our bright sun. All in fun, we call you folks the werewolves."

"Must you play drama queen, hon? Such a deplorable archetype," Mark said, when they had let Kate off at her trailer.

Her headache intensified, and back at the condo, she popped several more ibuprofens, went straight to bed, and fell into a deep ten-hour sleep.

❂

The next morning, she felt "off." Her head was still throbbing, and she had no appetite. She got up, and went into the kitchen to brew her coffee, a morning habit Mark disapproved of. He sat on the sofa, talking to someone. After five minutes, he hung up, and said, "Hon, I told Kate we'd meet for lunch."

"Please, Mark, I'm not up to it."

With a faint sneer, he folded his arms across his chest. "It surprises me you'd be rude. You, who's always so midwestern-nice."

"I'm not feeling well."

"I told her yes for both of us, and yes it is. Get yourself together, we leave at 11:30."

He was right, she told herself, her behavior was bad, and she had slipped into childish whining. Her attitude had been negative even before they had left LA. But still, a little sympathy from him would have soothed her.

*

The coffee shop was vintage 1970's. Dusty plants with curling brown leaves struggled to grow in cracked ceramic pots hanging from the grease-stained walls. They sat in a red vinyl booth, Mark across from the two women. Dark green duct tape covered gaping slashes in the vinyl. Orange polyurethane protruded from these fissures.

Kate devoured a grilled cheese sandwich and slurped a chocolate milk shake. Diane sipped mint tea, and nibbled on plain pita bread.

Kate turned to Diane and grinned. "I've got something to tell you, I didn't tell you yesterday because I didn't think you could handle it. I took you to a vortex. It's a place where our gods talk with their favorites through a hole in the heavens."

Diane glanced at Mark, who was frowning and picking at an alfalfa sprout salad.

Kate continued her explanation. "Rich Americans fly here and pay me thousands of dollars to show them the sacred places. I don't guarantee anything. They often get upset because nothing happens."

She turned to Diane again. "You, my dear, have a true spiritual gift, our gods singled you out to talk to you. Aloha, and welcome to our land."

She reached out her plump hand and patted Diane's arm.

Mark grimaced. He stretched over the table and lightly stroked Diane's cheek. "Hon, you are one in a million. I'm so happy that you finally get what Spirit is all about."

Diane did not respond. Her chaotic thoughts escalated into a mute diatribe against Mark. See, you jerk, I'm more spiritually advanced than you, even if I don't follow your goofy Age of Aquarius rules. I'm positive you sweet-talked

Kate, the way you charm me and all your patients and every woman you meet, and I'll bet you dollars to donuts you'll stiff her for her fee. I feel for Kate, she's an excellent guide, but I certainly won't offer to pay her anything.

That afternoon, Diane drew the Venetian blinds in the condominium, and shooed Mark away. "I don't want to spoil your vacation. But I told you I'm not feeling well."

Mark glowered. Without explanation, he left. Even though she felt abandoned when she heard the door close, still, his absence was a relief. Now she could sink into silence.

❋

Toward evening Kate's narrative shattered like a meteor into Diane's mind. There was a dark undercurrent to all religions. They had a way of turning suddenly and attacking a person's mask of sanity. She felt hot, flushed, unhinged. She tiptoed unsteadily into the bathroom to examine her face in the mirror. The color was a rosy red.

She splashed cold water over her face. The cool wet helped a little. This holiday was a disaster, worse even than her original forebodings. What was Mark up to? Suppose he and Kate were plotting against her, pulling off an elaborate hoax, snickering at her reactions? But her sixth sense told her that Kate would never participate in such a prank. Moreover, what if she was right about these local gods? They might decide to pick up and carry their favorites off to the other side. She stumbled back to bed. She thought of calling Angela, but the long-distance charge for the condo phone was prohibitive.

She couldn't recall when Mark returned. When she awoke the next day, still with a terrible headache, he was already dressed, preparing to go out. Sleepily she informed him she was not up to sightseeing. He took off, slamming the door behind him, and when he returned some thirteen hours later, he threw sheets and pillows and a blanket on the sofa, and bedded down there.

The remaining four days on Maui felt like exile. These were not the luxurious quarters of Bonaparte on Elba, but at least there were clean quiet rooms with blinds to keep out the sunlight. The wordless air vibrated with resentment. Mark repeated the pattern of going off alone, returning near midnight, and sleeping on the sofa. She laid down *Bleak House*, as the lengthy tale of a Chancery lawsuit was too convoluted for her to follow in her present befuddled state. Another novel was tucked inside her suitcase, *The Green Knight*, by Iris Murdoch. Already in the first chapters the plot proved bizarre, but no more so than the plot of her own real life stranded on this sinister island. Then again, she was stuck with the pedestrian name Diane. Why couldn't her mother have named her something chichi bohemian like Aleph or Moy? Several of her LA acquaintances had gone to court and changed their names, part of the process of "self-actualization," but she wondered whether this wasn't a kind of pretentious cheating. Each night she walked to the strip mall, ate at the vegetarian restaurant, and treated herself to a double-dip chocolate ice cream cone, but otherwise she stayed inside.

The final night, while packing suitcases, Mark confronted her, his controlled voice more intimidating than any yelling match could ever be.

"What's wrong with you? Epstein-Barr? Early menopause? I see women like you all the time in my practice. But I certainly would never be in a relationship with them."

"I know, something is wrong. I don't feel like myself."

"You should see a physician, have a complete battery of tests. You're not the same woman you were when I first

CURIOUS AFFAIRS

met you. You were a sexy babe. But you've changed into a drooping bore."

"I'm sorry. I can't put my finger on it. I'm sure I'll be OK when we get back to LA."

"I'm your lover, not your therapist. Get some help. I can't take it anymore."

There was nothing to say in reply.

They were uncommunicative after that. At the airport, the agent changed their seats so that they sat apart, he at the front, she at the back of the plane on the five hour flight. She did not see him deplane. Downstairs at the baggage claim, he was standing at the far end of the conveyer belt, chatting with a model-thin, tan, blonde woman, who pointed out a Globe-Trotter suitcase, which he retrieved from the conveyor belt. He stacked it together with his own suitcase on a luggage cart. Laughing, they walked off together. Wilting with fatigue, Diane caught the shuttle bus alone back to her apartment.

Thereafter, Mark vanished, as if their entire seven-month love affair had been a fictive dream. She was too exhausted to care.

❋

Now, Diane's funk deepened. She barely made it through her busy days. Every hour was crammed with the stop-and-go commute on the 10 Freeway, the nonstop rush of her job duties, frantic trips to Vons, to the manicurist, to the yoga studio, to the Jiffy Lube oil-change kiosk. She collapsed into bed every night at nine o'clock, exhausted. On the weekends, she had no energy to pursue her former activities: standing in line to see the latest foreign film at the Nuart, meeting her girlfriends for cappuccinos at the Coffee Bean, shopping the sales in the Montana Avenue boutiques for clingy silk dresses and costume jewelry.

She cancelled the standing appointment with Adolphe, her Melrose Avenue hairdresser. Her hair was growing in gray, and fell in a disheveled mass to her shoulders. She no longer visited the salon Precious Nails, where Lynn, a subdued Vietnamese woman, had buffed and polished her fingernails for the past fifteen years. She stopped going to yoga class. Her posture slumped, and flab formed around her waist and hips. New wrinkles emerged around her mouth. Loose folds developed in her once unlined neck, and brown spots appeared on the skin on the tops of her hands. She avoided any reflecting surface, bathroom mirrors and plate glass windows, and she removed the compact magnifying makeup mirror from her purse.

Messages piled up on her home answering machine. She checked them, but deleted them impatiently without returning the calls. Several of the calls were from Angela, but she never called her friend back. She had been proud of the cleanliness of her apartment, but now dirty dishes moldered in the sink and a layer of dust accumulated on the furniture. Dirty clothes spilled over the sides of the plastic hamper in her laundry closet. A heap of unopened mail cluttered a corner of the living room. She managed to open the bills, and perfunctorily pay them. An outsized Visa bill listing Maui expenses roused her to a mini tantrum. She pounded the table as she wrote out the check. Mark was a self-absorbed jerk, no, worse than that, a nasty beast. The anger soon subsided, and she hardly thought about him.

Once Gloria, who worked on a different floor, stopped by Diane's cubicle. All was wonderful in Gloria's world. She had finally met her soul mate in, of all places, an AA meeting, and they were moving in together. He was sixty, a character actor whose face everyone instantly recognized, though he wasn't a name. A lot of money in those bit parts, she was amazed to discover. He was a nice guy, many years married and now a widower, skilled in the art of pleasing and protecting a woman.

❉

On a Saturday night in early September, Diane reclined on the chenille sofa in her apartment. Her loneliness was palpable, like an icy bottomless black hole in the center of her gut. The atmosphere was hushed, silent, eerie from the fog. The Maui stone rested on the glass of the coffee table. She liked the Zen look of it, and its smooth gray texture.

As if prompted by a hypnotist, she got up, and walked into her spare room. Propped against the wall were stacks of cardboard moving boxes crammed with books from college. Preposterous, that she still had them. Her nebulous plan had been to buy bookcases to display them, but she had never gotten around to the project. She ripped off the masking tape that secured one of the boxes. The topmost volume was a scholarly tract titled *Origins of the Kabbalah*. As she opened the yellow pages, the binding split. The dust caused her to sneeze.

She walked back to the front room, and switched on a floor lamp with a Tiffany shade placed near the sofa. She sat down and opened the book. How puzzling was the explanation of zimzum, the contraction of the Deity before His creation. There were notations in the margins. The handwriting was her own. That other younger self materialized from the ether. The girl reclined, propped up on pillows on a plain single bed, in a tiny room on the second floor of a brick college dormitory in central Illinois, studying by the light of a goose-neck lamp. All was hushed. A north wind was blowing. The limbs of a massive oak tree outside the window creaked and groaned. Drifting snow had covered the window panes. The bells of Old Main campanile struck three.

Diane's eyelids fluttered and closed. The passage was too difficult. She had lost the scholarly discipline of that younger self. With her fingertips she traced the flower pattern of the chenille fabric. She laid the book down, turned out the lamp, and fell asleep.

Sometime later, she awoke with a start. Delicate moonlight etched shadows around the baroque carvings of the curio cabinet in the corner. On the coffee table, the stone glimmered and pulsed, phosphorescing with a bluish glow, and Hebrew script blazed on its surface. In some strange way she recollected the meaning, memorized by that earnest young female figure in a comparative religion class. The letters spelled out Ein Sof. The Irreducible Essence of God.

She reached over and touched the rock. It was hot, as if it had been steaming on an ancient altar over a sacrificial fire. As she studied it, she felt wobbly. A faint electrical whirring filled the room. It was muted, as if miles away, like the murmur in a conch shell, the illusion of a feeble echo of oceanic surf trapped inside the chamber of the shell. The whirring now crescendoed, full throttle, into the angry roar of a giant hive of bees.

Diane fumbled to switch on the lamp. The buzzing ceased abruptly, as if the light had chased it back into the fog-muffled night. The stone appeared plain, gray, unprepossessing. She touched its surface. It was cool, as cool as it was supposed to be, a normal gray rock.

What were the consequences of her innocent theft? She had purloined a rock from the Maui gods who surely had no power outside their remote island. How did these spirits know the God of Abraham, Isaac and Jacob? The Greek gods had punished Prometheus for stealing an ember. What sentence would they pass on her? Her head felt winched by a vise. With an effort she got to her feet, shambled into her small bedroom, and slipped into bed.

She awakened early. She padded in cotton socks into the front room and turned the handle of one of the casement windows. Moist fog swirled into the room. She pulled on jeans and a windbreaker. She picked up the stone, slipped it into the pocket of the windbreaker and walked down to the street. It felt good to breathe in the fresh, cold, salty air. At this hour, the entire world was enveloped by fog, and all was deserted, chilly, damp. She walked the twenty minutes to the ocean, meeting only one other person, a tall man who strode with a determined military bearing along the sidewalk at the edge of the beach.

She sat in the cold, wet sand, listening to the crash of the waves. A lone bombardier pelican swooped down to spear a fish. She took out the rock, and studied its contours. It was frigid to her touch. She placed her tongue on it and tasted salt. Salt, a primordial substance, the deep waters over which God had hovered, speaking the creation of the world.

What should she do with this object? Should she hurl it back into the ocean? And if so, which ocean? According to the globe of the world, the Pacific washed up on both the shores of California and of Maui. But what if the spirits were punctilious and exacting? A place for every sacred thing, and every sacred thing in its place. Should she mail it back to Kate, with an apology and a note as to where it belonged? But she did not know Kate's last name or address. Should she take a plane to Maui and replace the stone in the ocean? No answer came from the pounding surf, from the raucous cries of seagulls, from the drone of a jet overhead.

She returned to her apartment, and lay in a reverie on the sofa, sipping espresso thick with sugar. The stone lay on the coffee table, dull and unremarkable. Before retiring that evening, she placed the stone on her bed stand.

Sometime during the night, the Stone spoke in a baritone voice, echoing as if out of an underground cave. "My daughter, you are one of our favorites. The path is hard, it is terrifying. You have been sidetracked for many years. Should you choose to re-enter the path, we welcome you. It is good that you picked up one of our sacred fragments. Listen to us, and we will guide you."

The voice disoriented her. She seized the Stone, and pitched it into the sea. But it levitated on the surface, and grew larger and larger, its form more luminous, more diffuse, its round orb filling the sky.

She startled awake. A full moon filled the space of her bedroom window, its cold white light streaming in and lighting up the entire room. She lay in her bed studying the moon, the irregular patches of mountains and craters. The wind howled, and the windows creaked. The night clouds roiled and raced across the surface of the moon, and its light flickered, like a candle burnt almost down the whole of its wick. Soon, she nodded off again.

In the following three days, the Stone was quiescent. It no longer glimmered, nor did it speak. She carried the Stone to work in her purse. She would take it out often, staring at it, posing questions, talking into the air, as if to herself.

"Why are you quiet? Are you God's messenger? What really happened in Maui? What should I be doing?"

She brought the Stone under her quilt, sleeping with it, cuddling it. The nights were fitful. On Thursday morning, she called the personnel office, and put in a request for an unpaid leave, concocting a story about a family emergency.

The leave was granted. Management did not look favorably on such requests, but she did not care.

❋

And now, for whole days she lay on her sofa, paging through the book on the Kabbalah she had unearthed from the box, recalling as if in a dream the scholarly esoterica she had once known, and long since forgotten.

On a Saturday afternoon in early October, the kitchen telephone rang. Diane let the message machine click on. Angela was recording a message. On a sudden impulse, Diane ran to the phone and picked it up. How welcome Angela's voice was.

Angela said, "What's going on? Have you gotten my messages? Yesterday I finally called your work, and they said you were on sick leave. Are you OK?"

"I've been very tired. Since my Maui trip, last summer."

"And you and that psychologist—forgive me, I can't remember his name—you're no longer an item?"

"He hasn't called me in a long time."

"Ah well, you're better off without him."

The two women met for dinner that evening at Chung Huang, a neighborhood Chinese eatery, within walking distance for both. The place was a hole in the wall run by a disciplined immigrant family, and it was full. Clattering crockery punctuated the cacophony of animated diners. The walls were whitewashed, decorated with watercolors from China, depicting scenes of the countryside, ibises and water buffaloes in muted blues and browns. To one side stood an antique twelve-panel black lacquer screen, the pride of the patriarch owner.

Between bites of kung pao chicken and mu shu vegetables, Angela said, "I must be candid with you. You don't look well."

Diane took the Stone out of her purse and set it near the bottle of soy sauce in the middle of their table.

"I haven't talked about this with anyone. Do you see this Stone? I carry it everywhere, and it's disturbing me. Come back to my place after dinner, and I'll share the story with you in private."

Angela glanced at the Stone, a mundane, gray, round rock, nothing special. What was this puzzle? But always a good listener, she didn't ask Diane any questions there, in public.

They walked back to the apartment. Diane unlocked the door, switched on the Tiffany-shade floor lamp and the two Stiffel brass table lamps. She fussed over her friend. "Please sit here on the sofa. I'll fix some herbal tea."

She returned from the kitchen with two mugs filled with steaming chamomile tea. She placed the Stone on the coffee table, and sat in the brown leather armchair that faced the sofa. She took a centering yoga breath, then plunged into an introduction. "I need your honest opinion about something."

Angela rested her elbow on the sofa, her hand cradled in her chin. "I'm all ears."

Diane hesitated, and swallowed. "I've had certain, mmm . . ." She tried again. "I've had visions lately. I don't have a proper spiritual mentor to guide me, and even if I had, I would probably resist the help. Long ago I decided that religion is hokum, made up to control us."

"Go on."

She blushed and, crossing her legs, drummed her fingers on the arms of the chair. Her sweaty palms stuck to the leather. "I don't know if my imagination is working overtime, Angela, or if I'm having a nervous breakdown, or if in fact God may actually be speaking to me."

Angela was encouraging and said, "All of us see and

feel things. It's not at all unusual. Every human being has access to the divine."

Diane spilled out the story, barely pausing for breath. The priestess Kate, the roundabout trek to the lava flow, the frightening buzz, Kate's startling explanation. She pointed to the Stone.

"One night, a month ago, the Stone became hot and glowed in the dark. The letters of the Hebrew Mystical Godhead appeared on its surface. I heard the same terrifying drone of bees that I heard at the lava formation in Maui."

She stopped the tumble of words suddenly, as if applying the brakes to a runaway train. Angela sipped her tea, and placed the cup down on the coffee table. Her tie-dyed caftan flowed over an amorphous body; the room's oblique shadows softened the wrinkles in her round face framed by an unkempt gray 60s pageboy.

Angela's brow furrowed slightly. In a soft cadence, as if measuring each word, she said, "I can't give you advice, of course. But I'll share something in confidence with you, which may make your mind easier. I've never told anyone this before."

Diane said of course the secret was safe with her.

"The afternoon David died, I was in a faculty meeting. It was the year I was up for tenure. I could not afford to break any rules, or to be undignified in the presence of the department chair, who is an authoritarian from the old school. At 3:05, and I know because I glanced at the clock on the wall, I distinctly felt my spirit rise from my body. I soared to the top of the room, bumping gently against the ceiling. I looked down at the people below. One of those figures was my own body, myself."

She paused, searching for accurate words to describe the indescribable.

"A moment later, I floated down and re-entered my

body. I raised my hand, and interrupted the chair, a distinct no-no. I told him I must leave. The group stared at me, and exchanged baffled glances with one another. I walked out the door, got in my car and drove, propelled by a force I did not understand, to the exact scene of the accident one mile away, on PCH. The authorities later gave me his belongings. His watch was smashed, the time stopped at 3:05."

Diane sat transfixed, staring at her friend.

Angela said, "I don't know what my experience means. All I know is that I think a window into the divine opened for me that day."

Angela smiled, and then reached over and took her friend's hand. "Sometimes I get that same feeling from the literature I am privileged to teach, Eliot and Dickens and Trollope, all the Victorian greats channel the divine in their novels."

Diane squeezed Angela's hand and tears began welling up. "But, as you can see, the Stone has somehow depressed me. I feel crazy. I'm a mess."

"It's not the physical object. The Stone is only petrified lava. It's that the divine has pierced the usual veil, and is nudging you to change your life. It's not a one hundred percent change, maybe a slight readjustment, a two percent change will do. I have no idea what that change might entail."

"But why am I singled out to change? Other people are perfectly normal, oblivious to everything but making money and having fun. And *they* aren't hounded by strange buzzing gods and talking stones."

The two drank tea and conversed until almost midnight, when Diane drove Angela home.

❊

At five a.m. Diane drove several miles to St Monica's, a commodious Catholic church in the Spanish style, its bell tower crowned with red tiles. The interior was dim, not yet lit for early Mass. A homeless man, stinking of vomit, sprawled in a back pew, snoring loudly. She stood near a side chapel graced with a statue of Jesus pointing to His sacred heart, aflame with love for the world. So many years had passed since she had rejected those dead Latin formulas, the vocabulary of sequestered monks. But there was that wondrous idea, of boundless compassion and mercy, of divine energy available to all who would only listen to the small still voice within.

She felt somewhat better. Still, the thought of a full-blown Mass, the wriggling children and exasperated parents, the organ blasting full-pipe, was too much. She retrieved a bulletin from a table in the vestibule, and drove back to her apartment.

The bulletin called for volunteers to assist the Franciscan Sister Clare in her urgent mission to find shelter for battered women and their terror-stricken children. On the following Saturday, Diane pushed the intercom button at the charity's headquarters, a trailer parked in a vacant lot on a pot-holed street in Venice, the deserted stucco buildings tattooed with the graffiti of competing gangs, every window boarded up with weathered plywood. A rasping voice answered, and after Diane identified herself, the door buzzed open. A thin, no-nonsense nun of medium height grabbed Diane's hand and shook it vigorously. The nun's black eye-patch lent an impression of a fierce female pirate committed to kidnapping souls for the Lord. It was clear that no wife beater, even a ruffian with the bulk of a football linebacker, would dare to mess with her.

Soon it was an established routine to report to the trailer every Saturday morning to take calls from panicked women. And over the next month, Diane felt better and better.

Diane bought a delicate black lacquer stand in a shop in the Third Street Promenade. From the top shelf of her closet, she took down her box of special treasures. In the box were an intricate lace doily crocheted by her great-grandmother Alma, and a large rosary, its wood beads polished from daily use over a half-century. It had belonged to her great-aunt Sister Therese, a cloistered Carmelite. She fashioned a kind of altar, the doily draped over the lacquer stand, the Maui Stone circled by the rosary on top of the doily. This altar was the first object she saw every morning.

In the second week of November she called her hairdresser Adolphe. He threw up his hands when she crossed the threshold of his shop, and smirked at his assistant Yuki, who giggled.

"*Mirabile dictu*, what's happened to you? To the rescue, mademoiselle! Yuki and I will fix you right up."

After three hours under the hands of this master of disguise, there was her fashionable blonde self, staring back at her from the mirror rimmed with gilt seashell carvings.

Now at night she enjoyed the placid slumber of a cosseted housecat. Her looks had regained their pizzazz, and she returned to work, bounding through her days with the rhythm and discipline of a twelve-year-old gymnast. She was a regular at Sunday Mass, though she suspected that much of the dogma had been completely fabricated by argumentative neoplatonic philosophers. Somehow it didn't matter. All she knew was that during the recitation of Psalms and at the Elevation she reached for a tissue to dab at her tear-filled eyes. And she thrilled to the zenith of every mass: that serpentine line of respectful communicants winding its way up to the altar, each person's outstretched tongue fed by a priest, like a nestling nourished by a mother bird, a bland white wafer, the body of Christ.

Friends and acquaintances noticed a new sobriety, a new

thoughtfulness. The gossip in those circles was that something had happened in Maui, positively what nobody knew. Somehow Diane was not the same. Was it that she was not as coquettish, that her conversation lacked the old ironic deftness, that she was not in the know about the latest fashion trends? That wasn't it, not exactly. But all agreed that she was kinder, somehow, and gentler, and altogether a better woman.

Money Dragons

On a Saturday morning at eleven o'clock, Nancy sat at a vintage claw-foot oak dining table in her walkup apartment south of Pico. Her gray-streaked brown hair tumbled in a frizzled mop past her shoulders. She sipped coffee from a chipped mug while skimming the front page of the *Santa Monica Mirror*. A headline caught her attention: "Rash of Ellis Act Evictions Has Hit City." The article described the "ellis-ing," the forcible eviction of tenants like her who lived in rent controlled apartments. Thirty years ago her Aunt Shirley had found this crumbling four-unit stucco building through a woman in her church choir. Nancy's quarters were reached by an outside staircase of concrete slabs with a rickety corroded iron railing, open to the air and welded to the side of the structure. Inside, she had ripped out the avocado-green shag carpet to expose a dark oak-plank floor.

The orange marmalade cat, Puff, fat and in the splendid prime of his cat-life, pounced on her foot and then sped away. He jumped on the coffee table cluttered with well-thumbed paperback books bought at the library sales. Three were splayed open, face down, their covers plainly visible: *My Vast Fortune*, *Penny Pinching*, *Sylvia Porter's Money Book*. Puff crouched, expectant, his tail twitching, planning another attack. She had rescued him from a dumpster three years ago, a wee hungry kitten, shivering and mewing in terror. And why had she let down her guard? Every day she lamented the extra expense, and the chaos he introduced into her spare and methodical life.

She spoke aloud into the air, half to him and half to herself.

"You silly kitty, you don't have to worry about your next meal, at least not right now. You could do much better, you know. Fancy Feast every night and a jeweled collar. But you're from the gutter, and you don't know how to pick a richie mistress."

She startled as the doorbell buzzed.

"Now, who could that be?"

She peered through the security peephole in the front door. Her first cousin Susie, Aunt Shirley's daughter, stood on the landing. Nancy opened the door, and then the tattered screen door, which squeaked on rusty hinges.

"Well, I never, what a wonderful surprise," Nancy said.

The two cousins embraced. Nancy felt keenly how her own size-fourteen maternal midwestern plumpness contrasted with Susie's size-four California sleekness. Susie's face was flushed, and she glanced around uneasily.

"Sorry not to have called. I've got an appointment two blocks from here, and I thought I'd pop in for a few minutes."

Susie glided to the rose-pattern chintz sofa and eased herself down. Her denim miniskirt and black tights emphasized her lingerie-model-perfect thighs sculpted three times a week in sessions with a personal trainer. Puff jumped up beside her, and rubbed against her embroidered peasant top. She scooted away from him, and sneezed.

"Oh dear, I forgot you're allergic. Come here, pretty kitty, and it's off to the dungeon with you," Nancy said.

She picked up Puff, who clawed and struggled to break free. She deposited him on the bedroom floor and closed the door. From behind the door came the sound of frantic scratching and indignant meows.

"Can I fix you coffee or tea?" Nancy said.

Susie shook her head no, and Nancy pulled out a chair to face the sofa.

"It's been way too long. What brings you to this neck of the woods?"

"I've got a facial with Magda, who uses all organic herbs. I don't know why these holistic types insist on slumming it." Susie examined the five-carat diamond that sparkled on her left ring finger. Her face rimpled a little, and her eyes watered. From her allergies? Nancy wondered, wincing at Susie's insinuation that this entire area was a blight on the prosperous Westside.

"I can't stand it anymore, Nancy, I want out," Susie said finally. Tears dripped down her cheeks, and she removed a tissue from her Gucci matelassé handbag and dabbed at them. "My mascara is ruined," she murmured.

Nancy was taken aback. What could be troubling her cousin? Nancy owed it to her Aunt Shirley to be kind to Susie. Shirley had died four years ago from swift-moving ovarian cancer, and in the final hours Nancy kept an all-night vigil by Shirley's bedside. Shirley was only fourteen years older than Nancy, more a sister than an aunt. Nancy missed her terribly. It was as if her fairy godmother had disappeared and she no longer had any magic charms to protect her against the impersonal forces of this gritty metropolis.

Nancy mustered a casual tone. "What's wrong? I thought you were rich and happy at last."

"He's stingy. I can't possibly fix the house up with the little he gives me. I'm thirty-nine. He's my last chance."

Susie lived north of Montana Avenue with her third husband Eliot, an attorney who drafted contracts for A-list actors. Her first two marriages had been Las Vegas elopements. Two years ago Eliot had financed an "intimate" wedding at the Hotel Bel-Air. Nancy, as well as Susie's two brothers, had not made the cut for the guest list of seventy. The couple was renovating a "magical Cape Cod." Susie's sole job was to negotiate with an army of contractors and decorators.

"So divorce him. You'd get a nice settlement."

"He made me sign a pre-nup."

"You could easily find a good job."

"I have no computer skills. And I have zilch savings. Nada. I can't stand the thought of being poor."

"Poor is not the end of the world."

"It's just not fair. Why is everyone else rich, and not us?"

"Not that many people are rich. And there are a lot of people who drive leased BMW's who don't have even one thin dime saved."

"I'm scared. I don't know how to scrimp like you do. And I couldn't bear to live like this."

She grimaced as she surveyed the opposite wall. A water-stained poster print of Monet water lilies hung lop-sidedly in its plastic frame.

Nancy flushed. Resentment over Susie's rudeness bubbled up. If Shirley had been alive, Susie would never have dared exclude her from the wedding. And now, to be libeled repeatedly in her own sanctum. It was beyond the pale. But still, she owed Shirley so much. The older woman had invited Nancy to many Saturday night dinners, and she was always welcomed at Christmas and Easter and the Fourth of July. Nancy accepted, as the trip back to Illinois took almost a full day of travel time, and airfare that she couldn't afford to spend. She recalled Shirley's kindness ten years ago. Nancy had collapsed at work, doubled over with abdominal pain, and paramedics had rushed her to St. John's Hospital for an emergency appendectomy.

Shirley had driven twenty miles from her home, a rented adobe tract house in Van Nuys, to be by Nancy's side, and had insisted that Nancy recuperate for six weeks in Susie's childhood bedroom.

Nancy smiled a Mona Lisa half-smile. She would never bare her teeth. They were the color of old ivory piano keys. A small pointed peg tooth broke the line of the top row. She halfheartedly joked, "It's not so bad. Perpetual grad student, as they say. Except I'm not a real college grad."

Susie didn't respond. Her pink-glossed mouth pursed into a practiced sulk. She said, "Eliot's friends are so stuck up. They look right through me, like I'm not even there, like I'm Palmdale white trash."

Nancy sat silent. Why had Susie bothered to stop by? When would she leave?

"Look, here's the thing. I'm in a lot of trouble. I need two grand. I thought maybe you could help," Susie said.

Oh, so that was it. Phishing for dollars.

"I'm not a good person to ask. I barely make ends meet."

"You haven't saved a little? I'll pay you back, with interest."

"I have a small emergency fund. But I need every penny. And I'm scared because my rent may well go up soon. In fact, I may be evicted. You've been reading the papers?"

Susie shook her head no. She played with her mousse-tousled hair. Then she spoke, as if to anyone who would listen.

"I'm desperate. I need a quick abortion."

"What? Didn't you say last year you were hoping for a child?"

"I'm pretty sure it's not Eliot's. You remember Tom, my old boyfriend, the rock musician? I met him at a club, one thing led to another, and now, I can't believe it, I'm knocked up. If Eliot finds out. . . ."

Nancy frowned. Who was she to reproach her cousin? Unless a woman exercised vigilance, life could be messy. She remembered once missing a period, during a long-ago fling with a much older man. He immediately offered to pay for an abortion, which had been legal in California for several years before *Roe v. Wade*. Thank God she had not had to decide, because as it turned out, no actual pregnancy materialized.

"I'm very sorry. I don't have any money to give you. "

Susie stared at Nancy, a pout flitting across her mouth. Nancy remembered that look of Susie's, first as a sullen tweenager dressed in Jodie Foster *Taxi Driver* hotpants, later as a flirtatious Debbie Harry at the peak of her Blondie persona. The pout was now etched into a tiny wrinkle, a faint line of entitlement around her mouth.

The pout quickly was rearranged into a smile. "Please, cousin, you're my only hope. If mom was alive, she'd help me."

Nancy shrugged, and repeated that she was broke. The pout reappeared, then was smoothed down again.

"I know I've sprung this suddenly on you. I'll give you more time to think about it. I have a month or so left to figure out what to do."

Nancy said, "I'm sorry, the answer is no. But I hope this won't come between us. We'll always be family."

Susie said nothing, and got up to leave. Nancy offered to walk her to her car, and Susie did not object.

The two women strolled along the street. Three little girls, their faces smeared with chocolate, halted their rope skipping and watched them pass. Empty Coke cans and plastic bags littered the mousy grass. Gangs had spray painted graffiti on the mailboxes and traffic signs. Pods dropped by untended eucalyptus trees and fronds broken off from scruffy palms piled in the storm drains. Nancy tripped over asphalt chunks that had been upended by tree roots, while her elegant companion sidestepped all dangerous cracks with a natural grace.

At the shiny black Mercedes wedged between a sooty Honda Civic and a dented Chevy Tracker, Susie cursed aloud. In the brief thirty minutes, birds had dropped several glistening green and white guano splats on the Mercedes' hood. Crinkled brown leaves lay curled beneath the windshield wipers.

"Eliot is going to freak when he sees this mess. This bird crap can eat through car paint in an hour, and it costs thousands for a decent paint job."

Nancy pulled a crumpled tissue out of her pocket and spat on it. She rubbed the droppings, and polished the metal. Then she collected the leaves and tossed them back on the street.

"There, as good as new."

They hugged goodbye. Walking back, Nancy paused at the corner. The Mercedes lurched as it pulled away from the curb. The glamorous driver was laughing as she chattered into empty air, a hands-free phone on the console.

❋

Three weeks had passed since Susie's visit. Nancy stumbled out of bed. It was the first Saturday of the month, set aside for paying bills. She showered and pulled on faded gray sweatpants and a frayed white Hanes Beefy-T imprinted with the slogan "Be an Investor." At a financial conference five years ago she had stood for an hour in a line of blue-rinse–haired grandmothers to acquire this prize, worth almost fifteen dollars retail.

She scooped up a wicker basket stuffed with a jumble of envelopes that lay on the top of the black filing cabinet next to her bed. Opening the bottom drawer of the cabinet, she removed a manila file folder labeled "Net Worth." She settled in at her oak table. A shaft of sunlight slanted through the open window and lit up a luxuriant spider plant festooned with baby spiderlets sporting tiny white blossoms and spilling over the sides of an iron stand. Wind chimes tinkled softly in the slight breeze. The barking of a dog punctuated the squeals of a band of children. Puff sat upright and alert in the front windowsill, contemplating the view.

Scowling, Nancy brandished a cheap letter opener and slit each of the envelopes. Examining each bill, she spoke aloud, as if addressing the spiderlets.

"How could I have used three more therms of gas than this month last year? I must be more careful. I'll cut down on cooking. And what's this? I used twelve more kilowatts of electricity. Ouch, how did that happen?"

Her mind skittered to a thought that was worrying her. She muttered, "What if they evict me? Where could I go? Even Palms is too expensive."

She wrote the amounts on her plain blue safety paper checks, posted them in her checkbook, and glowered while subtracting each debit from the dwindling balance. Even as a six-year-old, she had saved her pennies and nickels inside her pink ceramic pig Porky hidden under her bed. Her parents bickered constantly about the household expenses. She determined to be different. Every night after her bath and before her mother kissed her goodnight, she counted her coins.

Her twenty-year-old self had been slim and pretty, proud and hopeful, traveling from her hometown Shawneeville, Illinois, to Los Angeles on the Greyhound bus, a faux-parchment diploma from Andrew Jackson Community College stowed in a hand-me-down beige Samsonite, the best typist in her class. A downtown law firm immediately hired her in their probate practice. Grim reality set in gradually. In her job she made just enough to get by. Through prodigious sacrifice she set money aside. In her twenties, she had two romances, one with a fifty-year-old married man, a litigation partner in the firm, who after one year—and that horrifying pregnancy scare—had abruptly told her it was over. Thereafter they pretended they had never even met, and avoided each other in the hallways. Thankfully he had retired some dozen years ago. The other love affair was with an accountant her own age who, after five years of dating, returned to his high school sweetheart. She began to stash candy bars in her home cabinets and in her work cubicle, and her weight ballooned by forty pounds. By her late thirties, it became apparent that she would never marry, and that her salary level was set in stone. The seven figure partners bragged about their pro bono work, but never shared their profits with the employees. Her only pension was what she had socked away in her 401K.

Now, one by one, she unsealed the fat envelopes from banks, mutual fund companies and brokerage firms. She worked for an hour, copying the amounts from the statements to a sheet of fourteen column accounting paper. Puff kept jumping on the table, testing his paws on her spreadsheet and purring, and each time she scolded him, hoisted him up, and set him again on the floor. She added the figures. A total net worth of $824,578, down a wrenching $44,067 in the past month.

"This market correction's a killer. I'll never have any security. And Puff, do you hear me, you're no help. You cost an arm and a leg. Seems you could catch a mouse once in a while, but no, I spoil you rotten." Puff licked her hand with his rough tongue.

The doorbell sounded. She dropped her pencil, grabbed the spreadsheet, and tucked it inside the manila folder.

The peephole revealed a thin, elderly black woman, stooped and out of breath, clutching a stack of *Watchtower* pamphlets in her left hand.

Nancy sighed. How could she possibly be polite to this intruder? She knew the lady was sincere. And, poor thing, exhausted from that climb up the cracked, uneven steps, and worn out from a life on the margin. But really, it was not her problem. And she was sick of these trespassers. Jehovah's Witnesses were a swarm of locusts, one of the many plagues of the low-rent district. They would never dare solicit her if she lived in Brentwood. Normally she hid inside until they gave up and left their pamphlets rubber-banded around the doorknob, but this time she decided to confront the woman head-on.

She opened the door and waggled her finger at the woman.

"Go away. If you don't leave, I'll call the police."

And now, the click of high-heeled booties. Susie was bouncing up the stairs, dressed in skin-tight Calvin Klein jeans and a low-cut breast-revealing spangled asymmetric tee. She pulled a twenty-dollar bill out of a crocodile hand-bag, and waved it in the air.

"Hello, dearie. A donation for the cause."

The old woman gaped. Her silver-blue curls quivered under her velvet cloche ornamented with iridescent green-black feathers. Muttering under her breath, she snatched at the money.

"Thank you sister. May God bless you and save your soul." She turned and began to totter back down to the sidewalk.

Nancy opened the screen door to let Susie in. As if scenting another lockup, Puff bolted outside down the stairs. A screak from the woman, now near street level, as her long black gabardine skirt became momentarily entangled with orange fur.

This melee was pure farce and Nancy couldn't help giggling, though Susie's return was unwelcome. It meant another appeal for money, no doubt. She hugged Susie, and the two cousins sat side by side on the sofa. Susie blinked back tears.

"It's twelve weeks already. You've got to help me. I don't know where else to turn."

"How about your brothers?"

"They're mad at me, we're not speaking. Eliot watches me like a hawk. He doesn't keep cash in the house. He lets me use his Amex black card, but he grills me on every charge."

She was sniveling. Tears streaked her mascara. She dabbed at her eyes with her French-manicured hands. Nancy noticed that one of the polished nails was visibly chipped.

The scene belonged on daytime TV. Susie's devoted fans would gossip delightedly about her predicaments in paradise.

"Please, please help me."

Nancy took her cousin's hand. "Your mother was very good to me over the years. But I simply can't afford to help you. I'm very sorry."

Susie stared at the wall.

"Do you have any Fiji water?"

"I've got Big K decaf diet cola in the fridge and ice from tap water. I know it's poison, especially now you have a baby to think about."

"I guess it's OK. Better than nothing. But no ice."

Nancy rose and walked past the table into the cramped kitchen. She retrieved a can of soda from the 70s-mustard-color Kenmore refrigerator, yanked the pop-top open, and removed a glass from the brown laminated cabinet. She turned around. Susie sat at the table, the manila folder open before her.

"Whose stuff is this?" Susie's voice was accusatory.

Nancy blanched. She felt faint.

"Please don't touch that. It's personal."

"This is your money, isn't it? And you pretend to be poor."

"Really, Susie, it's none of your business."

"I always wondered what you did with your money. You're such a cheapskate. You just stiffed that poor old lady. And you can't give me a lousy two thousand? What's wrong with you?"

Nancy's heart fluttered. This was a scene from her worst nightmare. Someone had stumbled on her secret. Now she would be hounded by the whole world. An imaginary Greek chorus rebuked her. Give money to the poor, help your cousin, you greedy rotten miser.

She braced her hands on her hips.

"Do you have any idea how much I've suffered to save my money? How hard my life is? No, you have no idea."

"And my life isn't hard?"

"You don't understand. You have Eliot, you have a gorgeous house, you look like a cover girl, and you can easily get someone else if Eliot doesn't work out. Men never look at me. I haven't had a date in twenty years. No one will help me if I end up broke. All I have is my money. It's all I have, all!"

Susie rose from the table.

"You know, I've always felt sorry for you, always felt like you were alone, with no friends. And everyone thinks you're poor. But you're filthy rich. After all my mother did for you, she practically adopted you, she treated you better than me. You, the hick orphan who ran away from god-knows-what cornfield. And I just can't believe you won't help me."

Nancy stared at Susie. Never had her cousin said such hurtful words. There was some truth to the accusation. Well, what if Shirley had liked her better than her own selfish daughter? Nancy had acted as a considerate and grateful sister to Shirley.

Nancy's voice rose to a Valkyrie shriek. "I'm not a tramp who needs abortions. This is your third, but who's counting?"

"Now you're judging me. How dare you."

"Abortion is evil, Susie, there, I've said it, I'm not religious, but some things are just plain wrong. Yes, I'm judging you, straight out, what you're planning is a horrible, unforgivable sin. I want no part of it."

"I'm a good person, not a creepy tightwad like you. I've raised a ton of money for Save the Children."

Nancy didn't hear this retort. She was now sobbing, her breast heaving like a child who has fallen and scraped a knee. Jagged monosyllables punctuated her gasps.

"I work hard every day of my life, scraping and saving. I don't need you. I don't need anybody. I'll do everything myself. Leave me alone. Don't ever come back here again."

Susie grabbed her handbag and stalked out. Nancy heard her heels clacking on concrete. A car door slammed, an engine revved up, and tires screeched.

❋

During the long afternoon, Nancy dozed on the sofa. Puff was constantly coming in, going out, coming in. After briefly nestling in her lap, he yawned and stretched and jumped to the floor. She stroked his back as he purred and rubbed against her hand. Again he went to the door, meowing loudly. She let him out. He did not reappear in time for supper. At about nine o'clock, she heard a faint mewing—not his usual raucous cries. And there he was, limping and bleeding at the bottom of the steps.

"Oh my gosh, what has happened to you, poor kitty? Goodness, it's going to be impossible to mend you. And I certainly can't afford a vet bill."

She clambered down and gathered him up in her arms. He lay still against her body. She settled him in the bottom half of a flimsy white cardboard sweater box.

"Hello pretty kitty, let me wash your wounds."

Puff hissed and growled at her. She gave up trying to nurse him, and left a plastic bowl of water near the box.

Should she take him to the animal hospital a mile away? She would have to call a cab, and the veterinarian would cost a fortune, especially on a Saturday night. His wounds looked serious. But after all, animals in the wild healed just fine without costly intervention. Surely he would recover after a few days.

She awoke early the next morning. The ocean fog was as thick and soft as angora wool. Puff lay on his side, his legs stiff, his head askew, his pink tongue peeking from his mouth. He was no longer whimpering, no longer breathing. The water bowl was untouched. A drowned cockroach floated on its limpid surface.

She sat on the sofa, and contemplated the body of the dead cat. She liked the handsome Puff, certainly. But she was not really a "pet person." What if she had taken him to the hospital last night? But of course, that was too expensive. No animal was worth that kind of money. She recalled a two-month battle between her parents when she was eleven, nonstop yelling and slamming of doors. The family's collie had sickened in early December. Her mother took him to the vet, and wrote a check for $600.

Her father announced at dinner that the stupid dog had wrecked the family's holiday budget. They did without a tree, and Santa's sleigh brought stocking stuffers from the dollar store. An undersized ham with mashed potatoes made do for Christmas dinner. The check bounced, and then in January the dog died. It was February before her parents cobbled together enough to reissue a new check to pay the vet. Her young self had concluded that pets spell catastrophe.

She should honor Puff in some way, but how? She wasn't good with death ceremonies. At Shirley's funeral, Nancy had stood up to approach the podium to deliver a short eulogy but, sobbing convulsively, had sat down again, and handed the paper to Susie's older brother, who read aloud the two paragraphs.

Perhaps she might imitate the custom of the ancient Egyptians who sheathed their sacred cat mummies in linen. From her closet she retrieved a grocery store box stuffed with remnants of ragged cotton T-shirts and torn sheets. With scissors she cut into strips a sheet decorated with faded pink and green tulips, and wrapped the strips around the carcass. She placed the corpse back in the sweater box bottom and set the top over the bottom. What to do next? Animal Control charged $50 to pick up a corpse. There was no open ground in which to bury it. Between the apartment building and the city sidewalk was a narrow dirt bed planted with hydrangeas. That would hardly do. She secured the make-do coffin with masking tape, wrapped it in a plastic bag, and lowered it into the dumpster in the alley behind her building. The cavernous bin was half-filled with plastic bags reeking of rot and buzzing with flies.

She slammed down the lid of the dumpster. "Rest in peace, pretty kitty. In a dumpster I found you, and in this dumpster I lay you to rest."

On Monday morning, she woke to the sounds of the refuse truck clanging through the alley. The red numerals of her bedside clock read 8:00. But how could that be? She never slept past 5:30. Where was Puff? He always woke her by jumping on her feet and nibbling on her toes. She moaned, remembering that he would never play with her ever again.

She showered and dressed. There was no problem deciding what to wear. Her wardrobe was straightforward and efficient: two black wool skirts, four cream polyester blouses and three black polyester sweaters, all plucked from the mishmash of the racks at Ross. Her two identical pairs of black leather low-heeled shoes had been so often resoled by Avedick the Armenian cobbler that he could probably send his beloved grandchild to private school for at least a week on the ten-dollar bills she had handed over the counter in his shop reeking of leather and machinery oil.

She walked several blocks to wait for the bus. Shiny late model automobiles whizzed by on Pico Boulevard. She stood apart from her fellows. Two tiny gray-haired Chinese ladies stood arm-in-arm, whispering to each other. A middle-aged Filipina in a nurse's uniform read the *Los Angeles Asian Journal*. A teenage girl held on to the hand of a four-year-old boy. His black eyes sparkled with mischief as he wriggled in her grasp. She scolded him in Spanish. Growing up, Nancy had seen only people like herself, who spoke a midwestern American English in the flat affect of the heartland. Over these many years, she had grown accustomed to the bewildering ethnic mix. But this morning, the babble of many tongues and the roar and fumes of the cars exasperated her.

She arrived at the office at eleven. She rode the wood-paneled elevator to the thirtieth floor, and sneaked through the back door to her cubicle. Her e-mail inbox held ten new assignments with deadlines marked urgent. At noon, the office emptied. She pulled out a small plastic bag packed with her lunch. She sat alone, nibbling on a tuna salad sandwich, yogurt and a brownie baked from Jiffy mix. The raucous laughter of coworkers returning from their restaurant meals unsettled her. During elementary school recesses, she had sat by herself on the edge of the school-yard while the others disappeared, giggling and whispering secrets as they skipped off to dribble away their nickels on candy and gum at Sam's, the corner grocery.

The week whizzed by, a blur in many identical weeks.

On the following Saturday afternoon, she lay on her sofa, reading a book checked out from the library, titled *Asset Allocation.* "Chapter 9, Portfolio Optimization." Her lips puckered, and she began to weep. Softly, quietly at first. Then hysteria roiled over her. How was she going to make it through this empty weekend? The hours stretched before her, with no Puff to amuse her. The break with Susie was complete. She hardly knew her neighbors. The office was a snake pit of gossip and backbiting. She was utterly alone. Of course she could always move back to Shawnee-ville, to that tribe of stolid peasants whose thoughts never soared, who could not imagine anything beyond the daily monotony of life in their bland cookie-cutter bungalows. By now her seven nieces and nephews had produced a gag-gle of fifteen snot-nosed children splashing barefoot in Chickasaw Creek. In all these years she had visited only twice. She knew her family through occasional photos, her three siblings already proud grandparents, her shriveled father wheelchair-bound, her white-haired mother hob-bling about with a cane.

How was she going to make it through the rest of her life? The pent-up loneliness of all these years of exile swelled into her body. She was weary, beaten down by the cramped habit of thrift. But there was no alternative. Those protective money dragons, the fierce guardians of her frugality, had turned on her. She was trapped inside a cave of fear with those monsters barring the entrance.

She said aloud, "It's not fair. Why doesn't anyone ever help me? Why am I so alone?"

A jet airplane droned overhead. A dog howled nearby, and another smaller dog began to yip, but no voice answered her.

Galileo's Finger

ON A GRAY NOVEMBER MORNING in 1979, Louise Stark, a plump American woman in her late thirties, stood shivering in a gallery in a museum in Florence, Italy. In her hands she clutched a decades-old Baedeker guide bought in a used bookstore in Chicago and a leather notebook with a Bic ballpoint pen clasped to the cover. Her frizzy auburn hair glistened with water droplets. A large wool paisley scarf was draped around her shoulders.

She had found the rusticated stone Romanesque building only by meandering around for almost an hour near the Palazzo Uffizi, up one narrow vicolo and down another. Morning mist had turned to a light rain. In a cloakroom near the entrance, an old woman dressed in black hunched down behind a marble counter. *The poor dear*, Louise thought, as she handed over a five thousand lira bill, and waved away the proffer of change. The woman smiled, revealing toothless gums, took Louise's damp umbrella and raincoat and placed them somewhere below the counter. She mumbled "grazie, grazie" and waved Louise inside, toward the gloom of the vestibule.

Louise trudged up a staircase of endless stone steps, to the primo piano, all the while puzzling over the word "primo." After all, it was really the second floor, and from the street it appeared at least four stories high. She walked into a room to the right of the landing. She propped her

leather saddlebag against the wall, removed from it the Baedeker guide and the notebook and pen, and began to circle
the room, studying the objects on display. A curious glass
egg attracted her attention. The egg was mounted on an
alabaster base. Around its middle was a ring of gold filigree
that covered a hinge so that the top and bottom must pull
apart like a clamshell. The base was inscribed with rhymed
verses in praise of Galileo Galilei. At first she thought that
a centuries-old fetus rested inside the glass egg.

Was the great man also an anatomist?

She studied a faded label, and translated the Italian as
best she could. The object was Galileo's right middle finger
bone. His bones had been exhumed and reburied inside an
elaborate monument at the Church of Santa Croce in 1737,
almost one hundred years after his death. A certain Signor
Gori, overcome with admiration for his hero, had detached
the finger bone and placed it in this ciborium to be revered
generation to generation. And then, fifty years ago, the Italian authorities had moved the ciborium to its present rest-
ing place in this room.

❀

Galileo's Finger rested in the glass egg and dreamed of the
years of glory. It had released cannonballs from the top of
the campanile in the Square of Miracles in Pisa while the
crowds buzzed with excitement seven stories below. It had
manipulated the lens into the telescope that first magni-
fied the moons of Jupiter. It had gestured to the Inquisition
judges as the scholar defended his theories.

The Finger had long imagined release from Its glass cas-
ket, and ecstatic reunion with the spirit of Its master. But
It had no opportunity to escape. Most guidebooks did not
even see fit to mention the museum. An occasional solitary

tourist drifted through the musty rooms, respectful but bewildered by the jumble of astrolabes and lodestones. Only a half dozen visitors in the last ten years had caught sight of the Finger. Invariably the traveler would gasp, and whistle in fascination or disgust. The Finger determined with all the strength of Its mind-force that the next pilgrim who lingered near the glass must, and would, be the vehicle of Its rescue.

And now, sixteen months later, Louise had appeared.

❀

She screwed up her face, concentrating on the object, trying to understand.

"Unbelievable," she said.

She had grown accustomed to the bones of saints set in jeweled reliquaries in the treasuries of the churches. The closer to Rome the bigger the bones. But the preservation of Galileo's Finger seemed a singular paradox, since his heresies had so disturbed the Church. Was the father of modern science now regarded as a saint with his finger on display for the faithful to venerate?

She stared at the Finger. In these last three weeks, a kind of traveler's fatigue had set in. She could no longer focus on the history of the city-states, on the names of the churches or the painters of the frescoes. The historical epochs were a muddle. Why had the Guelphs battled the Guibellines, and by how many centuries had the Etruscans antedated the Romans? She could not remember.

In her exhausted trance, it seemed to her that the Finger began to communicate. It did not speak out loud. All was silent save for the metronomic ticking of a humidity control device. But she distinctly heard Its urgent message.

"Luisa, bellissima Inglese, you are a lovely American

girl. You have a romanzo with the language and culture of Italia, with the soil of our fathers and the rose garlands of our mothers."

The baritone voice spoke in English with the aristocratic intonation of Professore Cosimo Ficino. Last January, she had braved the sub zero temperature to hear him lecture on 'The Harmony of the Spheres in Botticelli's Goddesses' at the Art Institute of Chicago.

"Do not be alarmed. Per favore, pick up this glass prison and rescue me. I wish to be buried in the soil near Arcetri where my blind master lived out his melancholic final days. I desire to decompose naturally and return to the earth. I do not want to be forever on exhibit in this orb, reverenced by my countrymen and mocked by foreigners."

Louise was by now tapping one short pink manicured fingernail on the notebook and fidgeting with the pen. She studied her own middle finger and wondered if some zealous Italian priest or government functionary might sever it. No, because she was an obscure American paralegal with neither saintly nor scientific predilections or accomplishments.

The voice of the Finger unnerved her. The rules of host country protocol had been breached broadside. A frugal traveler in possession of a blank journal and delusions of poetic talent relished the thousand discomforts that became the stuff of novels: maddening slow rides in bare third class railway cars; flea-infested beds in pensiones with Cararra marble floors; swarms of gypsy children in the Rome train terminal; the gelatinous eyes of a grilled fish on a dinner plate in Venice. But even the most intrepid tourist never expected to be accosted by a finger of a historical figure dead almost four centuries.

She stared at the Finger for several more seconds, and then she panicked. She did not dare address It directly, but turned her head and spoke as if to a companion.

"I seem to be losing my mind. I must go back. It's stifling in here."

She grabbed the leather saddlebag and bolted toward the door, banging her hip against a shelf and knocking over a set of brass compasses. They clattered with an eerie tempo, faster, faster, dancing a tarantella until they fell silent, abruptly, as an Apulian peasant might collapse, bone-weary after the strenuous revels of a village wedding feast. The room was again quiet.

The Finger now cajoled and commanded.

"Bellissima, my gorgeous madonna, my pet, you must, you will pick up the glass. It will separate easily from the alabaster stand. Do not be disheartened. The task is elementary. Place the glass in your pouch, and walk past the entrance portal to the street. I will instruct you further. I will reward you with the wealthy lover of your fantasies."

Louise shuddered. She glanced around, and peeked into the room beyond. Not a soul in sight, nor any sound of footsteps or voices. She snatched at the glass egg. It toppled off its alabaster base into her hands as if it had never been attached, and she almost dropped it. The glass was not heavy, and felt like the tiny bowl she owned as a girl, in which so many goldfish had perished from overfeeding. She wrapped it in her scarf and placed it inside the saddlebag. She ran out into the corridor, bounded down the stairs and sprinted pell-mell into the street.

The light rain had intensified into a steady drizzle. After a few moments her leather shoes were soaked with water. Only now did she recall that her raincoat and umbrella were inside the museum. She made an abrupt about face, almost falling as she slipped on the cobblestones. Her heart pounded as she re-entered the massive bronze front door and scuttled into the cloakroom. She set the saddlebag on the floor.

It seemed an eternity while she negotiated with the old woman. Her scant Italian failed her. She gesticulated with hand motions of pointing to sky and opening and closing. The woman scowled as she reached under the marble counter and produced the raincoat and umbrella. Louise fumbled with the sleeves of the raincoat as she jerked it over her body. She picked up the saddlebag and punched at the latch of the umbrella. As the aluminum ribs lurched and the mauve nylon canopy expanded she was already out the door, sloshing through deep puddles.

The street widened into a piazza. A tavola calda was directly opposite. She stamped her shoes and shook out the umbrella as she entered. The place was empty, save for a young girl with black eyes who stood behind the bar. Louise pointed to a glinting copper Cimbali espresso machine that covered half the wall. The girl approached the maws of the machine that whirred and shot thick black espresso into a white ceramic cup. She placed the cup on the counter. Louise stirred six lumps of sugar into the coffee. As she gulped down the hot sweet nectar she coughed, deep in her chest.

I must be catching a cold. But I simply can't allow myself to be sick. I'm so far from home, and I have to figure out what to do with this dreadful thing.

She pointed yet again to the machine. Cradling a second cup of espresso in her hand she walked over to a small table in a far corner of the cafe. She placed the saddlebag on the table, and sat down, feeling for the glass egg nestled in the scarf. Her heart fluttered.

What a nightmare. I simply must get out of this strange land and back home before I go out of my mind. I'll go to the Alitalia office at once. It will cost me an arm and a leg to change my flight. Geez, I'm up to my eyeballs in body parts. What should I do? Maybe I should return it. I feel so guilty.

I've never even stolen a stick of chewing gum. But I can't go back to that ghastly room or I might get arrested for shoplifting or stealing national treasures or God knows what else, and what if they throw me into the dungeons at Castel Sant'Angelo, like Cavaradossi, and they executed him by firing squad after he kissed Tosca goodbye, and he sang about her sweet hands, still alive, but then soon enough she leaped over the walls, only, oh dear, that's not a good example because it's only an opera and not real life.

Louise slammed both fists on the table and moaned. Yet again, came the coaxing voice of Galileo's Finger as from a cavern deep inside the earth, although It was only just inside the saddlebag.

"Bellissima Luisa, do not despair, you are my sweet angel and you have almost completed your dangerous mission."

Louise nibbled on her lower lip. She shouted at the bag. "Leave me alone, you monster. You're hideous." She glanced toward the espresso machine to see if the barista girl was watching. But the girl had disappeared somewhere.

"Do not be frightened, cara Luisa. You have undertaken this quest for the love of the unsurpassed culture of my beloved country. I know it is difficult for you and I have reconsidered. It is impossible for you to locate Arcetri because you dare not attempt a single syllable of conversational Italian although you have studied our excellent Dante so diligently while across the ocean."

Louise frowned. "Now you're insulting me. But you can't talk to any living Italians, either. I'm sure they would make fun of you."

"Ah, I treasure you, principessa, and I do honor to your singular American work ethics."

"I can't believe I'm even talking to you. You're only a stupid severed dead Finger."

"Ah, my lovely one, listen to reason. It is an incontrovertible fact that you have no access to a motorcar, and even had you such access, our haphazard traffic petrifies you. I would rest contented if you would board the autobus to Fiesole and bury me in the hallowed ground of the Teatro Romano. My master often ambled there on spring afternoons, where he meditated and dreamed and changed the course of history."

"No, no. I won't go to Fiesole."

"Cara Luisa, Fiesole is a gorgeous tourist attraction with a five star view much admired in your Guide Baedeker."

"Forget it, you hideous creature, I won't go back to Fiesole. Never, never. That's final."

"Melancholy remembrance of a prior visitation?" said the Finger.

"How did you guess? I walked there one Easter morning many years ago when I dreamed of becoming an art history professor before I married Andrew and he made me so miserable and nobody ever helped me and thank God he died or so help me I would've murdered him."

Louise's eyes were now filling with tears. She looked up. The girl again stood behind the counter, staring at her. Louise smiled, and pointed at her cup, as a sign to pour another. The girl shrugged and prepared another espresso in a clean cup. She placed the cup on the counter. Louise arose and retrieved it. She sat back down at the table with her back to the girl. Again the patrician voice, seductive, demanding.

"Listen to me, my precious girl. A wealthy man will desire you. You will live in a granite townhouse on North Dearborn, just as you always have fantasized."

Louise visualized the cramped apartment in the decaying west side Chicago neighborhood in which she hunkered down alone in life. It was startling that this Finger knew her secrets, those desires so near her heart that she never told anyone.

"How dare you pry into my private thoughts?"

"My cherished contessa, you must trust me that your dreams will manifest."

"You're ridiculous. Stuff like that only happens in romance novels."

"Ah, but your so-called reality is but a miasma, a collective hallucination. Have confidence in me, bellissima. I will protect you. I will shower you with gold florins and the love of a generous patron."

Louise contemplated the Botticelli Venus gazing out from a poster hanging crookedly on the wall.

"That's a joke. I'll never find anybody. I'll never be happy, never, ever. I'm resigned to it. Why am I even talking to you?"

"Darling Luisa, I adore you and had my master Galileo known you he would have suffered madly for you, with inexpressible and unrequited love-longings, even as the divine Dante idolized his benedetta Beatrice. I am requesting only the most infinitesimal of favors. I promise, if you transport me to the Teatro, and bury me, I swear to you, by the holy pigment formulas of the incomparable Raphael, fortune will shower her blessings and you will be deliriously rich and happy."

Louise scrutinized the serene poster Venus. Annoying, how blondely complacent these Renaissance females seemed. The Finger argued a persuasive case. After all, the severing and display of fingers was not right, and when in Rome, one ought not necessarily to do as the Romans do if it involved say, throwing perfectly respectable people to lions. This was an almost identical situation. But this was all nonsense. She must be coming down with a fever.

She opened the flap of the bag and whispered into the opening. "Stop it, please. Leave me alone. Please, please go away."

"Ah, bellissima, your mellifluous voice is enchanting. Do I sense your acquiescence? You will be rewarded, I promise you. Now, I will guide you to the autobus. You will experience a pleasant ride, ascending through fertile hills to the stupendo Teatro."

Of course it would be lovely to see Fiesole once again. She had been meaning to go back. Besides, what if the Finger really had the magical powers which It claimed?

And so, she picked up the saddlebag, left a five thousand lira bill on the counter (*that poor girl works so hard, and that machine looks impossible*), trudged to the Piazza Maria Novella, and boarded the autobus. She was the only passenger. Stepping to the back, she set the saddlebag down on the seat beside her. The bus lumbered five miles, up and up into the Fiesole hills, and stopped in the Piazza Mino, the main square, where she disembarked. The rain had cleared, and the façade of the cathedral gleamed in the sunlight.

She walked toward the Teatro on the hillside behind the cathedral. Near the entrance a group of twenty Germans stood silent, listening to the precise gutturals of their guide, a sturdy woman with clipped gray hair. Louise skirted them and clambered down a side aisle. In ancient times, devotees had sat rapt with attention on these stone seats.

At the bottom of the theatre she crossed the expanse of the stage. She strolled into a grove of evergreens that encircled its perimeter. She removed the glass egg from the saddlebag. Scooping up the damp mud she dug a hole six inches deep. The earth smelled of clay and moss. Thus had the earth smelled to the actors as they waited for their cues, their faces covered with the frowning mask of tragedy or the laughing mask of comedy.

She pried open the hinge on the glass egg and tugged the Finger free from a dab of plaster. She laid the Finger in the tiny grave, and covered It with mud and evergreen needles. *Rest in peace, oh Finger.* And what had Galileo said under his breath to the Inquisition judges? "Eppur si muove! And yet the earth moves anyway!" But it seemed to her that at that moment the earth stood still.

She placed the glass egg back in the saddlebag. She climbed up an aisle of the theatre, and returned to the Piazza Mino, where she sat for an hour, breathing in the cool clear air. Sunlight played on the orange tile roofs of the villas and the hills studded with dark green cypresses rising from the silvery green mantle of olive groves. Ah, yes, she saw as for the first time, the landscape that the Renaissance artists saw, as they painted the loggias in which their serene Madonnas sat, and in the far perspective, the lines clear and true to the vanishing point in the upper quartile of the canvas, these hills, these trees, this light.

She was famished after her great odyssey. Her chest seemed congested, and every few minutes she coughed. She felt an impulse to spend money, to rebel against the cruel strictures of her budget. She splurged on a hearty meal in a trattoria in the piazza. Each table was set with a white damask cloth and miniature pink roses in a majolica vase. She ate a dish of grilled chicken and truffles recommended by the waiter, and dipped crusty fresh baked bread in virgin olive oil. The waiter brought a bottle of Chianti with a black rooster label (*the genuine thing*). She drank the red wine, and its warmth settled at the level of her chest, soothing the cough.

❊

Five years later, on a Sunday morning in May, Louise reclined in a cobalt blue silk dressing gown on a flowered chintz sofa near the bay window of a townhouse on the Gold Coast of Chicago. She had shed thirty pounds and metamorphosed into a blonde.

Her attorney husband Steven sat in a brown leather armchair. He was sipping coffee from a Lenox porcelain cup and reading the *New York Times*. On the polished walnut table next to him she had placed a green faience platter piled high with cantaloupe slices, croissants, scones, clotted cream and raspberry jam.

He rustled the pages of the *Times*. "Sweetheart, look at this."

He pointed to a small item on page eighteen and handed over the newspaper. The headline read:

Galileo's Finger Last Catalogued in 1950
Disappears from Museum
Authorities Baffled
Official Heads Roll

"They apparently don't know how long it's been gone. Didn't you see it on a trip to Florence, before we met?"

Louise smiled her practiced Botticelli half-smile.

"Why, yes, I did. I'm sure I've told you the story before, darling, how I arrived back at O'Hare and collapsed with a 102 degree fever. A severe case of pneumonia. How silly of me to go traipsing about in the rain. But those were my salad days. It cost me two months' salary to go even in the off season."

"It's odd that they simply lost track of it."

"Of course that's Italy's greatest charm. The Italians focus on beauty, on pleasure. But they have no patience for cataloging things. How many treasures disappear only to surface hundreds of years later?"

She glanced over at the mahogany cabinet. A collection of Murano glass refracted the rays of the sun and cast rainbow fragments on the ceiling. The centerpiece was a glass egg encircled with gold filigree. She got up from the couch, sashayed over to her husband, and caressed his gray hair.

"Would you like more coffee, dear?" she said.

The Beautiful Lady

ONE MORNING just after sunrise in the Eastertide of 790 CE, the merchant Tarasios opened his stall as he always did on market days. The church of Hagia Sophia towered over this quarter of Constantinople, and its epic dome shaded the kiosks that lined the narrow cobblestone streets. His only child, six-year-old Theodora, played hide and seek among the cedar tables stacked with icons. She was cross-eyed, constantly stumbling and bumping into walls. She tugged at her father's robe and held up two gold coins.

"Papa, let me help today. I can tell a good coin from a bad. See, this one has a picture of the wicked Caliph of Baghdad. If I see one of these, I ask, please instead, for this other kind with a picture of our emperors or of our blessed Christos the Lord."

He beamed at her. Precocious, this child, so like her mother, his beloved wife Euphrosyne, who had died in agonized delirium before hearing the baby's first squalls. Well, why not let her try? Customers might find her irresistible.

Tarasios was a dealer in painted icons and ivory carvings, as had been his father and grandfather before him. For the last hundred years, those carping Iconoclasts had ripped out mosaics and torn down icons from the walls of churches. But now the regent Irene had cracked down. Three years before, her loyal bishops had met in council at Nicaea. Under her orders, they proclaimed that icons were not sinful graven images. To the contrary, such icons were holy objects to be blessed and venerated. The artisans rejoiced. Their workshops were humming with new orders.

Through all these twists and turns of official dogma, Tarasios only shrugged. What did he care about religion or politics? It was no skin off his back, either way, as long as the authorities left him alone to trade. The common people had never stopped buying his merchandise. The soldiers, with their ready money, were his best customers. They bought sacred objects in high fever and for high prices. Against all odds they hoped to ward off the accusing eyes of the severed heads they stuck on poles in the public squares and the angry souls of the bloodied, mangled bodies they dumped in alleyways.

The throng milled about, haggling and gossiping. Many stopped to admire the little girl as she pointed out the gold leaf on the polychrome and the intricate carving of the ivories. She charmed dozens of gold coins out of the hands of strangers.

At dusk, Tarasios set about closing up. Theodora wandered around among the trove of icons: Christoi, Virgin Marys, bearded patriarchs, archangels with rainbow wings. With her far-sighted right eye, she noticed a glimmer near the entrance to the alley. She walked toward the light. With her myopic left eye she made out a wood panel propped against the back wall. On the panel an artist had painted a Virgin cradling the Christ Child. Her kohl-rimmed black eyes stared straight out. The gold-leaf halo around her head glinted in the gloom.

"Papa, where did we get this beautiful Lady?"

Tarasios was busy fastening the shutters, and not paying her any mind.

She picked up the panel, half her size, and lugged it to the front.

"Look, Papa. Where did we get this Lady?"

He glanced at his daughter.

"My child, I don't remember buying this one. How could it have gotten in here?"

"Please, please let me keep her. I just know she likes me."

He smiled. He could never refuse her anything.

"Well of course, my little precious one. And where do you want to put her?"

He placed the panel inside a large protective sleeve of blue silk. They walked the two miles to their house, Tarasios carrying the panel in his right hand, and holding Theodora's hand in his left.

He set the icon into an alcove built into the wall of Theodora's room. Every morning, the little girl gathered clusters of pink oleander and purple bougainvillea that bloomed in bronze pots near the fountain in the center of the tiled courtyard. She arranged a bouquet in a terracotta vase on the alcove shelf, and dusted the icon with a white egret plume. On her knees before the icon she prayed for small things: that the geckos scampering over the walls would sit still so she could pet them, and for big things too: that her cousins would stop taunting her about her squint and that her father would marry a kind woman.

One morning, as Theodora nestled bougainvillea sprigs in the vase, she noticed drops of water trickling from the eyes of the Virgin.

"Why are you crying, beautiful Lady?"

She dabbed at the Virgin's eyes with her finger. The clear liquid tasted salty, like the sea. She rubbed the water on her eyelids. Its pleasant warmth tingled and soothed her.

At noon, father and daughter ate their meal of fava beans and dates on stone seats in the courtyard. Tarasios sat silent, frowning at the marble lions carved into the corners of the fountain. Theodora was used to his brooding, to his melancholia.

"Papa, listen to me. The beautiful Lady has been crying."

"What lady?"

"Our icon, our Lady."

"My dear, you're dreaming. Perhaps you saw the night dew gathered on the wood."

"I rubbed her tears on my eyes. I see better, somehow."

He was observing her now, his little one with the lively imagination. To his surprise, it seemed to him that her black eyes no longer wobbled, but gazed straight back at him.

"My child, you aren't squinting anymore. What if the icon. . . . ?"

He did not finish the sentence, but got up and walked into her room. Amazed, he gasped aloud. The eyes of the Virgin were crossed, the angle of their vision askew.

Tarasios immediately carried the icon in the silk sleeve, together with a woven basket filled with bread and fermented goat cheese, to Phosterios, the blind hermit. The merchant was in luck, for it was a visiting day. The hermit sat on a boulder just outside his cave. A long line of pilgrims filed past, kneeling and exchanging words with the holy man. Tarasios waited several hours. Finally, it was his turn. He knelt before the monk and whispered his story. The hermit listened, while touching the icon and stroking his long, bedraggled gray beard. After a few moments of silence, he raised the vacant whites of his eyes toward the sky, and held up his wrinkled hands, his arms shaking with palsy, his jaundiced palms facing out in blessing.

"You have sinned grievously. You are possessed by the demon of acedia. You have scorned the commandment to remarry. But this is a miracle, blessed be the Theotokos, the God-bearer, the all-holy Mother of God, and blessed be her holy child the Christos. Anathema to all heretics, to the Frankish barbarians, to the Mohammedans. You must praise God, Blessed Be He, every day of your life. Go in peace, and sin no more."

And so it was that from that day, Theodora's eyes untangled and she saw the world straight and true, as other children did. And the eyes of her icon, of the beautiful Lady, remained crossed. Tarasios soon married a lovely woman who embraced Theodora as her own. It is not recorded whether any gecko ever sat still long enough to be petted.

The family built a little chapel with a simple wall niche near the marketplace, and placed the icon in the niche. For many generations thereafter, the faithful believed in the miraculous powers of the Lady. With her far-seeing right eye, she watched over the entire city, and with her near-seeing left eye she recognized and blessed anyone who knelt before her.

Sappho Resurgent

Sᴜɴʀɪsᴇ ɪɴ ᴛʜᴇ Aᴇɢᴇᴀɴ Sᴇᴀ begins with red splinters striping the gray fog that obscures a midnight-blue sky. That's why Homer intoned "the rosy fingers of Dawn." Because it's really like that, Eos the dawn-goddess tiptoeing in her silken sandals, preceding the sun-god Helios who gradually turns the black hulking reptilian island-shapes to gray rock and silvery-green foliage.

It was in an odd giddy moment, on the sixth day of a twelve-day Aegean cruise, with Phosphorus, the huge morning star, visible on the horizon, that Barbara understood she was channeling classical Greek poetry. She leaned over the burnished brass railing of the cruise ship *Calliope*, and shouted into the wind, "An ancient Greek bard! Alive today!"

Her sister Marsha materialized beside her.

"What did you say?" Marsha said.

Barbara blinked, hesitating the tiniest microsecond, then plunged ahead. "I'm a lyric poetess, and passionate odes are welling up!"

Marsha frowned. "What's with you this morning?

Barbara suddenly remembered that she herself, Marsha's elder by two years, was the sensible one. Even a half-century ago in Albany when they shared a room, two single beds docked side by side in a sea of exuberant pink, Marsha had been the frilly giggly one, addicted to Barbie dolls and shirking chores, while Barbara had dutifully memorized the Baltimore catechism and kept her underwear and socks military-straight in the two dresser drawers assigned to her. To this day, she carried a rosary, often caressing the beads in secret.

"Oh, you know, when in Greece do as the Grecians do."

"What Grecians? The ones we've met seem down to earth, not airy-fairy."

"Well, OK, when in Greece do as Byron did."

"This is not good, whatever you're doing. You seem weirded out."

Barbara bristled. "Can't you let me play a little, the way I want to?

Marsha shrugged and pointed toward the front of the ship. "I need a bite of something. You should eat, maybe that would clear your head. Should we go in to breakfast?"

"Why don't you go in without me?" Barbara said.

Marsha winced, turned on her heel and disappeared. Uh, oh, Barbara thought, she's really mad at me now. Her surface politeness had begun to fray even on the first day of the trip.

Why couldn't it be easy between them, Barbara reflected, as she watched the sea-foam thrown up by the ship's engines, the ship transformed into Aphrodite's seashell. Her longed-for daimon had finally appeared, urging her to cast aside her humdrum life, to follow the secret overgrown path, that road-not-taken, of an artist. Her jokey comment about Grecians was a feint to stave off questions from her uncomprehending sister. But how (and to whom) could she dare communicate the pith of what she was experiencing? It seemed urgent, to transcribe on paper, and to declaim in public and for the entire world to hear, the Greek stanzas suddenly bubbling up inside her mind. Forget what anyone else thought. This included Marsha, who swam with elegant synchronized strokes in the conventional shallows of life.

"*Poikilo' thron' athanat' Aphrodita pai dios doloploka, lissomai se me m'asaisi med' oniaisi damna potnia thumon.*" Barbara chanted the uncanny syllables, not in the well-tempered scales of her beloved Bach or in the strict tempo of the Gregorian motifs she had learned as a child, but in an odd wavering nasal voice, the wailing tones and pitch slides she associated vaguely with Balkan folk music. And an English translation occurred to her, written out to be read, as if in an academic essay, which she burbled under her breath: "*Many colored throned immortal Aphrodita, daughter of Zeus, wile-weaver, I beg you with reproaches and harms do not beat down O Lady, my soul.*"

This was not going to be easy to explain, even to herself. She didn't know the first thing about ancient Greek, but these strange babblings somehow must be connected to that language, to that tradition of chanted poetry. How was it she intuited the English? And who thought or talked like this nowadays? How thrilling to have received this spiritual gift from unknown gods, but how alarming. Barbara had enough knowledge of Greek mythology to be wary of becoming involved with esoteric powers. She expected that Marsha's negative reaction was typical, and a good indication of how the world would judge her. She must hide this precious treasure away in a sealed Pandora-jar and guard the jar closely, unlike the feckless mythic girl who had released uncontrollable energies into the world.

❋

Odyssey Tours, specialists in Mediterranean travel, had slashed prices during the recession. The photos in the brochure had excited the sisters, who were both college graduates stuck in low-paying jobs, Barbara at San Francisco State in the dean's office (her major had been business) and Marsha at John Hancock Insurance in Chicago (her major had been art history). The sisters could have been poster children for a Norman Rockwell two-sibling nuclear family. They had been propelled into college by the grim discipline imposed by their G.I.-Bill–college-educated accountant father. Their mother was leery of the idea of college, as she suspected higher education of shaking the faith instilled in her by strict bewimpled nuns during her growing up years. Her birthplace was a small town in the Kentucky Holy Lands, populated by the descendants of English Catholics who had formed a league and migrated in the 1780's from Maryland to the wildwood frontier.

Only imagine, the sisters had enthused to one another on the phone, they could sail the wine-dark seas like Italian principessas. Two days in Athens, and then a magical cruise. The *Calliope* was a reconditioned yacht, spliced and diced to carry thirty passengers instead of one aristocratic couple. Neither sister had ever traveled overseas. Nor had they traveled together. This trip was meant to bring them closer, to repair the damage to their sisterhood that long distance and all their adult years apart had wrought. They never alluded to the vicious fights during their growing-up years, instead chirping to each other about how impossible their parents had been.

The two had flown on different flights, and checked into separate rooms at the Athens Plaza hotel. At the opening reception, they had twined their arms together and giggled like schoolgirls. However, after the first hour of meet-and-greet exclamations: "You don't *look* like sisters," Barbara began to wilt a little. The comparison deflated her spirits. Marsha expanded to fill Barbara's vacuum. During the next day of pre-cruise sightseeing in Athens—given over to the major sights—they were already drifting apart, Barbara always on the fringe of the group, taking careful notes in her Moleskine, Marsha amusing the others with racy comments: "Would you check out that nude statue's equipment, now there's an Apollo I wouldn't kick out of bed."

While meandering around the Acropolis, Barbara had exchanged tentative confidences with Robert, a seventy-ish man with a lanky six-foot frame topped with a shock of gray hair, bereft because his partner had died. Like her, he remained aloof, absorbed in his century-old, leather-bound Murray's *Handbook to the Mediterranean*, which, he boasted, he had picked up for a song at The Strand in Manhattan. Even though retired with the title of college professor emeritus in the department of English and American Literatures at Middlebury College, he continued his workaholic habits of nonstop writing and lecturing. He had disclosed that the purpose of this trip was to "get away" (from what, she didn't know exactly, something to do with a brouhaha that was roiling a gender studies section of the Modern Language Association) and that he avoided gay cruises because younger men were "brutal."

That evening there was no group event, and dinner was on their own. The two sisters walked around the block and ate in a small restaurant together. As they waited for their food, Marsha leaned in toward Barbara.

"Can we talk?" Marsha said.

Uh, oh, Barbara thought. Do I have to hear all this again? Marsha's mind moved in circles, always revolving around how to land a new husband.

"My stingy ex, sure he was generous to Amanda, she graduated without any student loans, but what about me? I'm the one who had to put up with his crap."

Barbara had always admired Kevin, and wondered how

he had survived Marsha's theatrics for fifteen years. Males were attracted to Marsha like insects to the sweet sticky moisture of the carnivorous sundew plant. Her slim figure was Elliptical-toned, her fingernails French-manicured, her toenails an iridescent bright pink, her hair professionally blonded and coiffed, her make-up applied over Botoxed skin, perfect as if camera-ready to do the weather on TV. A stern internal voice warned Barbara: stop this carping negativity. Be nice to your sister, she is all the family you have. She has her good points: self-discipline, social finesse, the occasional spasmodic generous impulse. Marsha had already presented her with a lovely gift, a pair of pricey gold Greek-key earrings. Marsha was thoughtful that way, always with an eye for workmanship, and eager to share her finds.

"I'm so sorry about your divorce. It's like a plague, everyone I know. . . ."

Marsha interrupted. "I'm just saying. My alimony checks have stopped, the deal was ten years, there's nothing to do, what am I supposed to live on? My ridiculous job pays me nothing." She was casting about for a lifeline, telling her troubles to some imaginary legal advisor in the middle distance.

"But you live such a glamorous life, I'm quite jealous."

"I've given myself a deadline—one year from now, I'll take my best offer, I've got three proposals, but every guy has a downside. The two with money can't get it up anymore, though that's minor, nothing a vibrator won't take care of. . . ."

Barbara was half-listening. She was mulling over why it was that they were so mismatched. What a waste Marsha's education had been. There was no sign of art history classes, other than an obsession with pulling together both her "outfits" and her "rooms."

At noon the next day, the *Calliope* sailed from Piraeus, the Athens harbor. Ever mindful of her budget, Barbara was squeezed into a lilliputian cabin on the Daphne deck, in the bowels of the ship near the bone-rattling vibration of the engine room. She had applied a scopolamine patch, which her doctor had assured her was fail-safe protection against seasickness. Marsha, who liked her comforts, and who, Barbara feared, had nothing saved for the future ("the future" terrified Barbara) was two levels up, on the Leto deck, in a spacious cabin with a large window, a queen bed, and a dressing table with a lighted cosmetic mirror.

Yannis, a muscular bearded crew member native to Mykonos, showed Barbara to her cabin. Flashing two gold teeth, as he lingered outside her open door, he had exclaimed that she was the most beautiful woman he had ever seen. Startled, beginning to panic, she firmly closed the door, mumbling a polite "thank you." At age fifty-six, a plump 165 pounds with a rosy complexion, Barbara never attracted men back home. Even when she was younger, she had never mastered the art of coquetry. This was one of her regrets, that she had failed utterly to learn a skill that came naturally to Marsha, and to most women, that art that began so early, of four-year-old Shirley Temples dandled on the knees of doting fathers and uncles, of prepubescent Lolitas teasing smitten, bewildered boys.

That afternoon, the two sisters attended tea on the upper deck, a Greek interpretation of the traditional British affair: unfiltered black coffee instead of tea, baklava in place of scones, yogurt a stand-in for clotted cream, and wild thyme honey replacing marmalade. Yannis hovered nearby, coffee *briki* in hand.

"This is unreal," Barbara said. "It feels like a dream."

Marsha was nibbling on a flake of filo pastry and paying no attention to Barbara, but smiling vacantly at the other women, and with effervescent come-hithers to the men.

That first night aboard, at Marsha's insistence that social hours are the whole point of a cruise, Barbara had drifted over to the lounge after dinner. The slightly aggressive drunken conversations disturbed her. Lots of fishing for personal information, sizing up relative status, raucous jollifications. It also made her nervous to be signing drink tabs. She suspected the prices were inflated, and to settle the bill at the end would be a shock. Since then, she had settled into her cabin directly after dinner, snuggling into the minuscule bed, studying, preparing for the following day. She wanted to know everything, to understand everything, though she could not say exactly what her goal was. Marsha had huffed, why are you so antisocial, no wonder you never find anybody, but by the second day she had given up. It was just as well; there was no help for their lack of harmony. The two made a pact to sit at separate tables at meals, agreeing that this was a good strategy to mingle with the other passengers.

❁

And now, Barbara remembered breakfast. She descended the short flight of stairs to the dining room. Marsha was nowhere in sight. She must have finished eating already. Yannis, in his white uniform with black shoulder stripes, grinned at her. Averting her eyes, she concentrated on the selections at the buffet. She piled scrambled eggs, cantaloupe slices and two poppyseed rolls on her plate, and dolloped plain white yogurt into a small bowl. Robert was sitting alone at a corner table, and she made a beeline for a chair next to him. Starting in on her eggs, she broached the topic now uppermost in her mind.

"Robert, did you ever learn Greek?"

His thick gray eyebrows, smeared with reddish-brown hair dye ill-calculated to make him look younger, twitched. He focused his myopic hazel eyes directly on her.

"Of course, my dear. In my undergraduate career at Harvard, a mastery of Greek was essential. Be that as it may, all those requirements have been consigned to the dustbin."

"Is there some way I could learn Greek quickly? Not living Greek," (she glanced across at Yannis, who was circulating among the tables serving potent coffee, and who immediately saluted her with his *briki*) "but classical."

"I am afraid that would require a prodigious outlay of time and energy and money. And of course it would be necessary to possess an elevated intelligence quotient, a minimum of 140." He examined her skeptically as he said this.

Barbara hesitated. The question was urgent, and he could perhaps help her. The words spilled out, all in a rush. "Do you think it's possible to channel ancient Greek poetic rhythms and somehow translate them into English?"

Robert picked up a fat orange and began to peel it with his bony fingers. The blood-red flesh and pungent aroma evoked an ancient vista, a white marble temple on a hillside in Lesbos. How she longed to loll among the columns, sharing a tangelo with a bronzed, lyre-strumming Alcaeus.

As he continued his methodical removal of the orange peel, she realized his words might wound her, and blushed slightly.

"Really, my dear, these California ideas are delusional in the extreme. Channeling? As I say, a concept embraced by village idiots. I would hope you are at least intelligent enough to avoid such nonsense."

Barbara looked to her left out a large porthole window. A calm blue sea stretched to the horizon. In the near frame, a promontory of bare rock glided by. How comfortable she would feel living on that rock. If the sea could not understand her, at least it was uncritical, neutral toward all creatures.

"*Let fruit be crushed on fruit, let flower on flower, breast kindle breast.*" A vivid image, a grove of almond trees in full fragrant blossom, languid bumblebees buzzing among the branches. Blue butterflies fluttered in a nearby field shimmering with yellow broom. A fantasy, of course, but so entrancing, so different from the daily grind back home, the tiny apartment in which she hunkered down alone, the bus ride to work, the monotonous routine of her dead-end job.

She rose from the table, muttered, "Excuse me," and straggled out. She felt sick at heart. If even Robert, immersed as he was in literature, could not understand her, how could she communicate with anyone at all? In the corridor stood Marsha, studying the day's schedule.

"Hey, sis, there you are. Seems we'll see a bit of Turkey today. How exotic is that?" Marsha's smile flickered out as she looked at Barbara. "Hey, are you OK? "

Barbara managed a shrug. "Oh, I'm fine, it's nothing really."

"I'll share my news, promise you'll keep a secret. You know that lawyer, Steve, the one from Boston? I think I can land him—at most two more days. Of course, that witch from Philly, what's her name Donna, she's throwing herself at him. She's been married three times, her family is loaded, posh office buildings."

Barbara recoiled. Really, they were completely incompatible.

"I'm so happy for you. He sounds perfect. I'm going back to my cabin to get ready. See you in a bit."

She descended to her cabin. Her stack of books rested

on the end table: two guidebooks and five books on Greek history and art (she had allowed herself to purchase them, at discount on Amazon) and also the *Landmark Herodotus* paperback. This collection had tipped her suitcase weight to two kilograms over limit, but the Lufthansa agent had waived the extra charge. She had also checked out two books from the ship's library—a political history of the Mediterranean, with numerous maps and illustrations, and a recent book by Michael Schmidt, *The First Poets: Lives of the Ancient Greek Poets*. Was she the last remaining reader on earth not to embrace the e-book? but she enjoyed the physicality of paper, of bindings, of marking her progress with artsy bookmarks. The scent of books calmed her. She had spent countless childhood summer afternoons wandering among library stacks.

She shook off her sandals, and still in her windbreaker and jeans, nestled in the disheveled bed. An enigmatic child's voice had urged St. Augustine "Pick up and read." Something more interior than a voice—an odd, hard-to-place feeling, some kind of fleeting premonition—led her, absentmindedly, to pick up the *Lives*. The book fell open to Chapter XII, "Sappho of Eressus." Fascinated, she began to read, at first skimming, then slowing down, savoring the blend of biography and analysis of the ancient poetry. All of it fragmentary—elusive facts, allusive lines of verse in an Aeolic dialect. She recollected, somehow, what exactly? It seemed to her the lines she was hearing must be those of Sappho. How she knew this, it was impossible to puzzle out.

❈

Fifteen minutes before schedule, at 9:45, the *Calliope* docked at the port of Datça, on the mainland of Turkey. The Greek guide, thirty-year-old raven-haired Ariadne, who resembled nothing so much as a willowy goddess on an Attic vase, shepherded her twenty-five charges off the gangplank and into a dented dusty red bus. Barbara and Marsha sat together in the front, Barbara near the window. One seat behind them slouched a pensive Robert, deep in corrections of the galley proofs for his latest article, "Sodomy Transformed: Aristocratic Libertinage during the South Sea Bubble."

The bus creaked slowly through the motor scooter- and pedestrian-clogged stone streets of Datça. Their destination, Ariadne explained into the microphone, was the site of the ancient Doric city of Knidos. The city experienced "a great flourishment" (Ariadne spread wide her arms)— renowned for the "pornographical" nude statue of Aphrodite by Praxiteles, and the "astronomical" observatory of Eudoxus. How peculiar, Barbara thought, that this place had ever been Greek. Signs in Turkish were jumbled one atop another, and numerous slender six-story minarets jutted into the sky like rocket ships poised to launch into the Muslim heavens.

The bus clunked laboriously up a narrow blacktopped road through mountains that unfolded a vista of gleaming sea and pine forests. Barbara watched the panorama, and, spotting a huge soaring bird, touched Marsha's shoulder.

"See up there. Some kind of wondrous eagle. Maybe Zeus himself, come to reclaim this land."

Marsha was snoozing, her head limp against the seat back, and did not open her eyes.

Barbara poked her head over the seat back and addressed Robert.

"Did you see that eagle? A sign from the gods. This is miracle ground."

Robert said "mmm . . . uhhuh," but remained engrossed in his proofs.

There was no point in addressing anyone else. She sank back into her own thoughts. The moving visual feast outside the window delighted her, all the details of the landscape were familiar, somehow, and she felt eerily that they constituted some originary place.

The bus lurched into the entrance to the ruins, past a small stone guardhouse, and halted in a parking lot with a stone concession stand. The two sisters stepped out of the bus. A strong wind, the prevailing northern meltemi, pummeled them.

"Yikes," Marsha said. "This dreadful wind will totally nuke my hair."

Barbara was barely listening. She stepped away from Marsha, and yelled into the wind.

"*Elthe moi kai nun, chalepon de luson ek merimnan, ossa de moi telessai thumos imerrei, teleson, su d'auta summachos esso. Come to me now, the harsh worry let loose, what my heart wants to be done, do it!, and you yourself be my battle-ally.*"

Marsha scowled. "Okay, I've had enough. Whatever game you're playing, stop it, please."

Ariadne motioned the group toward an amphitheater, a rubble of granite building blocks and marble pillar fragments. "I will organize the tickets. Meet me over there. I will give you directions, and then you may wander at your leisure."

Marsha grimaced. "I hope this doesn't take very long. Where in this god-forsaken place are we going to get a decent lunch?"

The group wandered over to the amphitheater, some perching on stones, others standing. Ariadne joined them, and began speaking into her microphone. It was difficult to hear her, as the blustery wind, combined with the crash of the waves on the rocky promontory of Cape Crio a quarter mile away, sounded like the roar of a Cyclops. The October air was chilly. A relentless sun beamed down, the tingling of a stealth attack of sunburn. Marsha fidgeted. As soon as Ariadne concluded her remarks (whatever they were, Barbara could not make them out), Marsha rebelled.

"This is not working for me." She pointed toward the concession stand. "I'm going to rest in the shade over there. I'm going to complain to Odyssey Tours. This whole side trip is ridiculous."

Barbara ignored her. "*By the cool water the breeze murmurs, rustling through apple branches, while from quivering leaves streams down deep slumber,*" she harangued the stones.

"Oh for crying out loud. Stop it. I mean it. You're getting on my nerves." Marsha stalked off.

Robert walked over to Barbara. "This is most extraordinary, this meltemi wind, the 'bad tempered one.' Of course I have known of it, but not until today have I comprehended its meaning."

Barbara, distracted, said, "Bad tempered? Are you talking about Marsha? She's usually not this way, except sometimes her anxiety . . ."

Robert interrupted her. "Really, my dear, you must pay attention to your surroundings. The brilliant Eudoxus founded a world-class academy of mathematics and astronomy here in this very place. And so, shall we explore together? Over that hill."

Barbara felt quashed. How she admired professors, how she quavered before them, fearing they dismissed her as a groundling. But she steeled herself, and followed him.

At the crest of the hill, they gazed at the sea below, in the near view a clutter of Doric columns prone on the ground amid granite stones overrun with a riot of purple and pink and yellow wildflowers. Everywhere lizards darted, flashes of iridescent green disappearing into the cracks between stones.

Barbara stretched her arms to the sky. "*Without warning, as a whirlwind swoops on an oak, love shakes my heart.*"

Robert smirked. "My dear, as I have explained repeatedly to you, with directness, albeit with gentleness, I am available to you neither for tryst nor yet for dalliance. Much less am I what my horrible vixen sister Carol refers to as marriage material."

Really, his pedantry bordered on satire, like a Saturday Night Live sketch. She suppressed a chuckle because if she showed even a whiff of amusement there was no guessing how venomous he might be. But wait, didn't she know this man from long ago? He must have been somehow in that other life, the Sapphic one. Had he been so condescending to her then? No, it was impossible. She was a rich and famous laureate, the acclaimed muse of young poets. She stared at him, and then her polite facade cracked.

"Stop it! Why are you so rude? My words are the very stuff that poems are made of! Don't you recognize them? I thought you were a genius, but you're only a pompous jerk, and, you're the, you're the . . . the silliest man I've ever met! You remind me of a scarecrow my dad set up in the back yard—the crows cawed and made fun of him and pecked out all his straw."

Robert's mouth literally dropped, as the expression goes in bad novels. "Well, my dear, the bad-tempered wind must be affecting you. This flash of rage is most curious. Pray tell me, have you ever sought competent professional assistance for anger management?"

Barbara glared at him. Why was it that reality never remotely approximated her favorite reverie, that other people were kind and intelligent, and appreciated the civil give-and-take of philosophical conversation? But to quarrel with him, to take her focus off this marvelous and somehow so-familiar landscape, and this intoxicating wind, was a waste of time, unless she could turn their argument into dactylic strophes.

"Don't you understand? I'm Sappho, and you'd better stop insulting me. I promise you, I'll get my revenge in a poem."

Robert studied her face. Then he pointed into the far distance.

"I cannot make out the sense of these ruins. Most disappointing not to understand. At a minimum, it is necessary to have a world-class private guide with an Oxford classics degree."

"Why are you changing the subject?"

"My dear, I believe it is time to reconnoiter with our colleagues at the bus. They will be expecting us."

"If you 'my dear' me one more time, I swear I'll . . . I'll—" Barbara could not think of what she might do. "OK, leave, but I'm not going back yet."

Robert glowered. "Very well, suit yourself," and he began climbing down the hill.

"*Although they are only breath, words which I command are immortal,*" she shrieked at him. Salt tears welled up, and dribbled down her cheeks.

※

That night, the *Calliope* voyaged westward, its destination Santorini, some twelve hours over open sea. Captain Aristotle, a short burly Athenian in his fifties, promised an early arrival at the old port in Skala Pier, 500 feet below the clifftop town of Fira—a special privilege, because the ship was small, and he had cousins there. Ariadne chimed in with speculations about the lost continent of Atlantis. Barbara watched the sunset alone on the upper deck. She felt alienated from Marsha, from Robert, from her fellows on the ship, from the whole world. Fragments of verse free-floated in her mind, as she watched the foam-wake change to golden, then red, and then begin to sparkle silver from a full white moon illuminating the violet waves.

She retreated to her cabin, to prepare for tomorrow's excursion. Instead of searching for material on Santorini, she took up the *Lives*, and continued reading the Sappho chapter. She already knew everything in these pages, though they were not things she recalled learning. And even more unsettling, she could have interpreted and expanded the material, easily and effortlessly wowing a roomful of scholars, even as the self-confident aristocrat Sappho had impressed the most arrogant of the Sophists who considered her the equal of Orpheus, the mythic poet who had mesmerized all living creatures.

Ten o'clock was Barbara's usual "lights out," but that night at about nine o'clock the *Calliope* began to toss in choppy waters, the swells cresting fifteen feet. It was impossible to read further. Nausea. Her scopolamine patch wasn't working. She wobbled unsteadily to the bathroom and threw up all her dinner. This was just as Homer describes the wrath of Poseidon, when the vindictive god seizes his trident and shakes up the sea. The waves crashed, and the ship rocked and swayed. Tell it to the marines, her somber father had repeated over and over, and so she, the first-born child, was always brave and uncomplaining. Probably Marsha was in the bar, laughing off this turbulence. Marsha boasted about frequent weekend sails on Lake Michigan with a "special friend." It wouldn't occur to her that Barbara might be suffering.

A poem-fragment came to her. *Death is an evil. That's what the gods think. Else they would die.* She teetered back to bed, and retrieved her rosary from the nightstand. Fingering the crystal beads, she began to whisper the mysteries of light. Surely the Virgin would intercede for her.

Barbara heard a faint knock on the door. In her delirium she imagined it might be Yannis. The door was locked, wasn't it? The ship pitched again, and she lay ashen-faced in bed, unable to form a sentence, even a feeble "go away." Then she heard the turn of the lock and the door opened. Good heavens, the crew had keys. She braced herself. Surely he was harmless, and nothing bad would happen.

The light switched on. A slender young woman stood in the doorway. Ah, now she remembered. It was Maricel, the maid, who every evening turned down the bedsheets, and left a chocolate mint on the pillow. Barbara was in the habit of answering the door, accepting the candy, smiling and wishing the young woman good evening. Maricel had mentioned a husband and two children in the Philippines (photos on an iPhone had been produced) who waited patiently for her while she was away four months at a time. Cruise ship gigs paid good money. Now she clucked sympathetically, and rang for chicken broth, ginger ale and water crackers.

"God bless you," Barbara whimpered. This lovely girl must be a deep-sea ox-eyed Nereid, riding to the rescue on the back of a Knossos blue dolphin. The Virgin had listened.

Barbara's sleep was fretful, and she awoke often. In her nightmares, the ship sank, and all perished except for Yannis and Robert, who floated off together in a lifeboat on a serene sea, a school of bottlenoses porpoising around them.

❄

In the morning, the sea was calm. Maricel brought plain toast and chamomile tea. At eight o'clock the *Calliope* was pulling into the old harbor. The passengers stood on the foredecks, ooh-ing and ah-ing: a deep lapis blue sea, from which rose sheer brown-black volcanic cliffs, at the summit whitewashed buildings that glittered against an azure-mist sky. Barbara, her head aching, kept to herself, watching from the lower deck. Over the intercom came Ariadne's voice, asking everyone to line up. The company had arranged a private pass to board the gondola and bypass a long line of tourists. They filed off the gangplank. Barbara was last, apart.

Marsha was chatting with a tall, tan man who was traveling alone; no wedding ring, and no white stripe where a wedding ring should have been. Barbara remembered that his name might be Alan, or was it Michael?, and he did something mysteriously lucrative on Wall Street and was constantly shooting photos with professional camera gear. From the look of it, Steve had not panned out, but this new one was an even better catch. Marsha's white-veneered teeth glimmered in the sunlight as she waved at Barbara.

Robert sidled up to her.

"Good morning, my dear. A most pacific and beauteous day, the proverbial calm after the archetypal tempest. Were you dispirited during this most protracted night of dread?"

Barbara could hardly form the usual banal response, Oh it was nothing, I must have slept through it, or some such. Rather, she said in almost a whisper:

"*Stand up and look at me, face to face, my friend. Unloose the beauty of your eyes.*"

He seemed not to hear her. "Sit next to me, my dear. This felicitous funicular will transport us to the apogee of this mythic volcano. A fabled civilization on the isle of Thera blown to smithereens."

But what was he pontificating about? It didn't matter, at least his voice and manner were friendly. She couldn't expect anyone to understand her. She stepped into the gondola seat. The machine clanked and swayed up the cliff face, dizzying vistas of blue-on-blue unfolding before them. Nausea again. She closed her eyes and recited several Hail Mary's, her lips fluttering.

At the top, she tottered out of the gondola, and sank down on a stone bench. Robert drifted away to the far side of the square. Marsha had ratcheted up her flirtation with the tall man. He had a casual hand on her shoulder, and was smiling, pointing toward the sea.

Marsha led her new conquest over to Barbara, to make the introduction. The name indeed was Alan.

"I haven't seen much of you," he said to Barbara, glancing quizzically at Marsha. "You don't look like sisters at all . . ." his voice trailed off.

Marsha took up the slack. "Oh I know, everyone says that." And teasingly, to Barbara: "A little rocking last night, just like sailing on the Lake, what fun, really."

Barbara did not get up from the bench and merely prattled the minimal niceties. "So lovely to meet you. What a perfect morning for walking." The A-list photogenic couple wandered off. Alan had slipped his arm around Marsha's waist.

Ariadne hallooed, summoning everyone to follow her. Barbara stood up. Thank goodness, her dizziness had lessened. The guide led them through the narrow pebbly streets, on schedule for a "special private visit" to the archeological museum, before the doors opened to the public.

Barbara lagged behind. She didn't feel like paying attention. Things seemed hopelessly muddled by the time they were filtered through Ariadne's quaint, accented English. She slipped around a corner into an alleyway, a winding cobblestone path perhaps three feet wide, between the smooth whitewashed walls of stone houses. She glimpsed intricate stairways, leading up or down to cobalt blue doorways. Purple and pink bougainvillea cascaded from walls and twined around windows. The alleyway meandered up, and at its highest summit dead-ended into a terrace with a plashing fountain in the center. A dozen patrons, a motley of tourists and locals, in their groups of two and three, relaxed at wooden tables under turquoise patio umbrellas at a little café connected to the terrace, plates of baklava and cups of sweet, strong *variglykos* set out before them.

After the shade of the alleyway, the sudden intense sunlight in the open terrace confused Barbara. Dizzy again, she collapsed into a chair at one of the tables. The umbrella shaded direct solar rays, but still the vibrant whiteness disoriented her. A young black-eyed black-haired waitress appeared. Ariadne had sworn by the healing properties of mountain shepherd's tea, though the *Calliope* didn't stock it, since the beverage was brewed from some unappetizing weed. Here on this menu it was listed, and Barbara whispered her order. The waitress brought a steaming cup and a plate of crusty bread. Barbara sat, dunking the bread into the hot yellowish liquid. The taste was citrus and mint, and oddly calming. There was a memory stirring of some other time, when this health-giving tea had been a daily habit and her creative energy unbounded.

Her head thrummed. *Phaon frequents the far fields of Typhoeus's Etna: passion grips me no less fiercely than Etna's fire.* Ah, yes, in that faraway time in college, her one fierce love, Dennis, whom she had seen French-kissing another girl on the quad as she returned from the library at ten p.m., closing time. She had never confronted him, but broke with him immediately and cried herself to sleep for six months. She was blushing to think of it: that semester had been the one blot on her college record. Straight A's except during the Dennis fiasco, when her record was sprinkled with B's and C's, and her chance at Phi Beta Kappa vaporized. And then her fervid determination to make it on her own. A woman needs a man like a frog needs a biology class full of seventh graders.

All these years she had relentlessly scheduled her life: nothing frivolous ever interfered. It was all work and keeping a spotless apartment and running to buy necessities, with a rigid bedtime and wake-up alarm, her only solace in books—but even then there had been reading goals, so many pages per day, so many books per month, a voice that lectured her if she didn't keep up the pace.

"You finally can rest. Relax and let go, Barbara." From somewhere, a consoling voice.

This long-deferred and longed-for trip was supposed to be exhilarating as well as educational. What was happening to her? Why these crazy thoughts, why this melancholy? And now a wailing melody, something unstable and disturbing, a chthonic lament quavering in harsh half-tones. *If you wish to flee far from Sappho of Greece, you'll still find no reason why I'm worthy of being shunned. A harsh letter might at least speak that misery, so that death might be sought by me in Leucadia's waters.*

Barbara rose from the table. She waved to the girl, handed her a ten euro note, and mumbled, "The change is for you." The girl's face registered a surprised delight with the American tourist's generosity, and she skittered back inside the café kitchen, as if afraid that her customer might renege. Barbara stepped over to the stone barricade, barely three feet high, which circled the terrace. She gaped at the picture-postcard view. A sheer cliff. Dark volcanic rock plunged hundreds of feet, at its bottom a thin strip of black sand and then an infinite expanse of cerulean water. Dazzling. Dizzy, impossibly dizzy. Her stomach roiled, as if protesting the strange herbal infusion that only the locals were used to, and an acrid minty taste filled her mouth. She leaned over the parapet, silver waves stippling an unfathomable blue expanse of primordial sea, bluer than any blue envisioned by even the most intoxicated of Impressionists. *Aphrodite, born from the sea, offers the sea to lovers.* Let go, finally, for the first time in your life, relax and let go.

None of the other patrons noticed Barbara's fall, so fluidly a part of the natural landscape, a croquet ball rolling down the gentle incline of a manicured lawn, Icarus gliding soundlessly into the sea as in the Brueghel painting, a ploughman and a shepherd oblivious. At four o'clock, when she didn't check into the ship, the alarm was raised. About an hour later, local fishermen found the body, still intact, blue eyes open wide, the mouth in an ambiguous smile, floating in a shallow lagoon a mile from the harbor, striped crabs already nibbling.

Beef Medallions

Fetus floating in the womb.
Do you know 'twill be your tomb?
Feel the cold steel suck and slice.
Where to hide from Hell's device?
God made you with holy breath.
Silent scream: can this be death?
No harm in it. Life so brief,
Shrug it off. But now, cruel grief
Like slow poison steals and seeps.
See this mother howl and weep.

SALLY TURNED ON her cell phone. Three messages from her husband Phil. She called his Century City office, and he answered.

"Oh there you are sweetheart." Was there a hint of annoyance in his unfailingly polite tone?

"Sorry, honey. I forgot to turn on the cell. There was a lovely sale at Citron, then I met Marisa for a long lunch at 17th Street Café, you remember her, my old girlfriend from high school? She's in LA visiting, you met her that one time, what, twenty years ago now, she couldn't make our wedding."

Odd to be lying to him, and especially to be embellishing the story with such petty details. Nothing to hide, really, and yet there was a certain verboten topic.

Phil said, "You remember my client Richard, from Disney. He and Irene have separated and he's a little lost. I invited him over for dinner, and we'll leave here in an hour. Drop by Whole Foods, would you, and pick up some beef medallions we can broil, and some nice sides. Hope you don't mind such short notice, I'll make it up to you, I promise."

"No worries, darling, there's nothing to make up. Dinner will be fun."

It was February, and an overcast sky threatened rain. She walked slowly to her BMW parked in the lot of St. Monica's Roman Catholic Church. She had driven there in a daze, and knelt in a back pew, head in hands, shoulders jerking convulsively. After a long time, she had stumbled toward the front, and collapsed into a pew near a side altar, close to a statue of the Sacred Heart of Jesus, votive candles sputtering in the shadows. The sanctuary was empty and silent, though every so often other solitary worshippers glided down the aisle and knelt for a while near the high altar.

It was the thirtieth anniversary of that blizzardy day she had crept into a storefront clinic, already at fifteen weeks, near the deadline for a no-questions-asked D&C second-trimester abortion. Afterward she had taken the bus home. The bus stop was a half-mile from her rental, two spartan rooms in a decrepit Edwardian mansion in Champaign, Illinois that had been carved up into units. The short walk exhausted her further. Shivering from the cold, she fumbled with the door-lock, and once inside, collapsed onto the sagging single bed. For the better part of two days she lay in a stupor, curled up and alone. She had told no one. Not her mother, not her sister, not her Aunt Alice, certainly not the father, a finance graduate student she had slept with on two occasions, who had stopped calling her, and whom she had never seen again.

About that time, she abruptly stopped attending Mass, and had never approached a priest to confess the sin. She had kept the secret even from Phil. Every year, on the anniversary date, she found herself slipping into a Catholic church in the early afternoon, praying to whom she knew not, for what she knew not.

And now, she stood at the meat counter in Whole Foods. The clerk was a young man, younger than her son or daughter would have been. A thirty-year-old grainy sonogram of a human fetus, light gray tissue against a black background, was tucked in a yellowing envelope inside a Stuart Weitzman shoebox high on her side of the walk-in cedar closet. The young man picked up three rosy-red medallions, and displayed them to her, proud of their quality.

"They are perfect, thank you, I'll take them."

The young man weighed them, wrapped them in white paper, and handed them to her.

"Have a good day," he said as she walked away from the counter. She wandered to the deli section. It took her a good twenty minutes to pick out several side dishes, fashionable carbs of yams and quinoa and bulgur.

She drove the two miles to their home, a Georgian style mansion north of Montana, graceful pines and eucalyptus lining the street, *Architectural Digest* perfect. She walked into the kitchen, Caesarstone and copper gleaming even in the gray gloom filtering through the skylights, and placed the medallions and the sides in the built-in SubZero fridge. Absentmindedly, she wandered down the hallway and turned into Phil's home office, where there was a view of a flagstone patio hedged by azalea and camellia bushes. The azaleas, wintry plants, had begun to bloom, and for a week she had been contemplating the gradual amassment of white and pink blossoms.

On Phil's immense walnut-burl desk was a display of

professional photos of the happy couple, taken at their Ritz-Carlton wedding fifteen years ago. At that time they had agreed that children would complicate their affairs too much. After all, Phil was forty-five and she was thirty-nine. He had two teenage daughters from an unhappy first marriage. Sometimes she wondered if this had been the correct reasoning, if it was why her abortion at twenty-four was still such a vivid memory. It wasn't simply the guilt. It was more than that, a feeling that she had foregone her one opportunity to become a mother. The announcement that Phil was to become a grandfather—his elder daughter was pregnant—had only reminded Sally of her own discarded fertility.

Phil was an outstanding husband, in many ways a perfect husband, a respected attorney and a good provider, a kind and thoughtful man. Her friends often remarked on how lucky she was. And yet. Something essential was missing from her life. It had to do with her core, her center, those early memories of candles lit for the Latin Mass, of caressing her blue-glass rosary beads, of memorizing the Baltimore catechism. This sophisticated persona she had assumed—a Pilates-toned body, hair blonde-highlighted and cut in cascading layers—in some mysterious way it did not represent who she really was. The scared child inside her was curled up in a freezing attic corner, hugging herself and crying.

It was past time to pull herself together. Mechanically she dressed in a sleeveless, floral, silk shirtwaist and gold wedge sandals, touched up her hair with a curling wand, and applied makeup. Phil approved this sleek, yet modest look, the glammed-up hausfrau who didn't embarrass him with tarty cleavage or Cleopatra eyeliner.

Two automobiles pulled into the driveway. Car doors slamming, baritone voices. She walked through the foyer and opened the front door.

Phil stood there, grinning. He stepped forward and kissed her full on the mouth.

"Sweetheart, you remember Richard."

Smiling, she gave the obligatory Hollywood hug and air-cheek-kiss to their guest. The arc of her arms was polished, perfect. But in fact this far too casual physicality dismayed the demure Catholic girl inside her.

"Welcome, come in. I'm afraid dinner will be hodge-podge pot-luck."

"Oh, my favorite kind. How generous of you to take pity on a poor unhappy bachelor."

There was a slightly inappropriate leer in Richard's manner. Maybe a few glasses of pinot noir would help her sleepwalk through the evening.

A Day at Versailles

"Sweetheart, look in here."

George pointed through the bottom panes of a pair of casement windows twelve feet high. The two Americans stood in the overgrown moss at the back of the Petit Trianon, the chateau of Marie Antoinette in the park at Versailles. Although the façade of the Greek revival building and its formal gardens presented a postcard-perfect public view, on this hidden side the walls were crumbling and the foliage had grown wild and entangled. Strangely, the glass panes were clear, as if recently cleaned.

Karen shaded her eyes with her hand and peered inside. The room sparkled. Gold inlay glistened on fresh-painted ecru walls and the polish of the parquet floor gleamed. A young woman clasping a leather book reclined on a velvet cushioned Louis XV settee. The flounces of her Robe à la Polonaise cascaded to the floor in waves of pastel green silk. Her chestnut hair fell in ringlets over her shoulders, almost touching the mounds of her breasts, which were pushed up by a tight corset.

It seemed the sophisticated French were taking a page from the corny Yanks, using a student to act the part of a historical figure. Karen giggled, remembering her high school stint as a tour guide at a landmark Victorian house. The museum board required guides to dress in character. Her assigned garment was a purple silk bustle gown, on loan from the local light-opera company. How she had loved playing the role of a fashionable lady whose monied family had built the mansion a century ago.

"Isn't that model exquisite, George?" She touched his arm. "She looks just like the Lebrun portraits of the queen we saw this morning."

"The French do things in style, don't they?"

"They certainly do. The ensemble is true down to every detail. But the hairstyle is wrong. Too many ringlets."

"It's odd that they would assign her to sit in a building closed to the public. Maybe she's practicing. Or perhaps this is a break room."

Turning back to the path, Karen noticed a marble lion head set into a collapsing stone wall, above a cracked basin meant to catch the water that dribbled out of its jaws. Peculiar, she thought. Lions were not the usual motif in this park. The unkempt brush gave way again to neat gravel as they rounded the building and came out at the front. They sat down on a stone bench near the entrance. The autumn weather was cool and sunny, perfect for dawdling.

The couple had stolen away from Chicago to Paris five months into their love affair. George was fifty-five, a seven-figure partner in the estate administration practice of a LaSalle Street law firm. Four years ago he and his wife had divorced, a surprise to the wider world, which glimpsed only Photo-Shopped monogamy. The actuality was different: he had dabbled in several back-street affairs, always breaking off when a woman became demanding. His wife had never discovered these infidelities, though she surmised that his long and irregular hours were not taken up solely with billable time. She had been preoccupied by the upkeep on their Evanston colonial mansion with its manicured lawn and expanse of gardens, and by jockeying for admission to elite schools for their two sons, both now grown and doing well in Silicon Valley. He was enjoying his new role as a desirable bachelor, photographed often with women at charity events, posing with this one, a bejeweled beauty or that one, a wealthy divorcee.

The never-married Karen was forty-five, and worked as an assistant curator at the Art Institute. The job seemed glamorous, but the reality was gritty for those like herself who had no trust fund to augment the meager salary. For the past two years, she had dipped into her scant savings for sessions with Dr. Ira Sand, a psychiatrist and Jungian analyst, who saw patients in a book-lined consulting room in an Edwardian row house near the Lake. In that hushed dimly lit room, its high ceilings softened by acanthus moldings, a Persian carpet covering the center of its polished wood floor, she sank into reverie. If only. If only she had grown up in a house with a room like this, and her father had been bearded and erudite and soft-spoken. Her own father, who had died a decade ago from a massive heart attack, had been a clean-shaven and hard-drinking Marine sergeant-major, barking orders to her mother, his second wife, some twenty years younger than he, and to her, their only child. He considered reading a waste of time, as so much navel-gazing, when there was real work always to do, to maintain a rigid structure and attend to every detail.

In April Karen had manned a booth at a charity auction of nineteenth-century British watercolors in the Gold Coast Room at the Drake Hotel. George attended because a client had donated a painting, and he took the opportunity to size up the women as well as the art. Pleasantries were exchanged and a flirtation ensued. She scribbled her personal cell phone number on the back of her business card and gave it to him.

They had arrived in Paris on a Sunday afternoon in September. George was paying for everything for this week-long getaway, his treat in lieu of an opal ring she had pointed out to him in a Magnificent Mile shop window. He agreed the ring was lovely, but had immediately changed the subject, nuzzling her ear and whispering, sweetheart, let's go to Paris together.

Karen had lodged briefly in a shabby Balzacian pension in Paris many years ago when she was traveling solo, Eurail pass and passport tucked into a neck security pouch, guidebooks and extra panties stowed in a backpack. George had been some half-dozen times on family vacations, staying in an apartment in the Trocadero owned by his former father-in-law. The first two days they lazed about, taking late breakfasts of baguettes and café au lait in the Hotel Saint Germain-des-Pres dining room, lolling abed during the afternoons, strolling in the boulevards at dusk.

On Tuesday evening, however, Karen, who in spite of Dr. Sand's calming influence, was jittery over the waste of even one minute, announced they should be on a proper tourist schedule. Versailles was first on her list. George replied that while he was happy to oblige her sightseeing whims, he would prefer another quiet day at the hotel. But he agreed it would be an easy trip, very little time or trouble. And so, early that morning, they had walked a block to the Metro. George took charge of the complex map illustrating the transfers for Versailles. During the forty-five minute ride on the RER train, Karen studied her Blue Guide. He rested his hand on her thigh, his fingers absentmindedly caressing her while he stared out the window.

The morning had been taken up with exploring the palace. After a light lunch of quiche and salad and a carafe of the red vin de table in the palace's mediocre café, they had idled in the park, and wandered over to the Petit Trianon to take a cursory look.

Now, settled on the stone bench in front of the locked building, she nestled against his shoulder. They were examining the neoclassical façade.

"It's wonderful, really, the elegant simplicity of this chateau. Rather a treat after the over-the-top gilt of the palace," she said.

He nodded in agreement. "The mob did not see Marie Antoinette's virtues. We see them now, two centuries later. She seems the sanest of the lot."

"She was a liberated woman, one of those brainy Habsburgs. Much smarter than her dolt of a husband, the sixteenth Louis."

Smirking, he said, "We Americans refuse to sympathize with the plight of any queen, no matter how brainy. We always cheer for revolution. Of course, they went a little overboard with the guillotine."

A tour group approached. Well-heeled Americans, Karen guessed, anorexic-looking women in skinny jeans and rhinestone-trimmed cashmere sweaters, their men in British-style travel vests over tailored shirts. The guide was a tall, slender woman wearing a gray sweater dress with a patterned red silk scarf draped around her shoulders. She stopped near the entrance. Scowling, she checked the gold watch on her wrist several times, while waiting for stragglers. After a few minutes, all two dozen people were gathered around her in a ragged circle.

"As a special surprise for you alone, our most distinguished guests, follow me inside, *si'l vous plait*." Her English diction was formal, with a thick French accent.

She opened the front door with a brass skeleton key, and led the group inside. Karen and George stood up from the bench, whispering to one another whether they could join in, and holding hands, latched on to the tail end, following them through the door. No one objected.

CURIOUS AFFAIRS

The interior consisted of an enormous high-ceilinged salon, empty of furniture. On the left side, was a marble staircase; only three steps were visible before its upward sweep was curtained off with muslin sheets. The group gathered around the Frenchwoman, who briefly expounded on the building's history and explained that this was the ground floor, relegated to servants and armed guards. She concluded, "In seven months this very beautiful, very important chateau is scheduled for restoration to the luster of 1789, when the magnificent queen Marie Antoinette resided here."

She then crossed the salon, the heels of her black leather pumps clacking on the marble tiles. On the far right, a door was set into the wall. She unlatched it with another key.

"You now have ten minutes at leisure. Through here is an old billiard room where the guards relaxed when off-duty. You may examine it, if you wish. I remind you that donations to assist in restoration projects are always welcome." She glanced at her watch, clacked back across the salon to the front door, and disappeared outside.

The Americans milled around. Some of the men took photos with expensive camera equipment. The visitors murmured in soft voices, or else were silent. One loud voice punctured this decorum: that of a woman, her neck and face surgically tucked, with hair dyed the color of orangutan fur and fingers flourishing diamond and emerald rings.

"Hey hon, they oughta dust better in here. Look at that filthy floor. You'd think they coulda hired better help."

Karen cringed. She imagined herself cheering as the sharp edge of a guillotine silenced those vocal chords forever. She wasn't sure if George had heard. He had the ability, honed by many years as an attorney, of tuning out obnoxious clients and colleagues.

The billiard room indicated by the guide must be the

room with the actress, who even now was probably fluffing her curls, getting ready to primp for the visitors. Curious, Karen walked to the right and stepped through the open door. The air changed abruptly to the cold clamminess of an underground crypt. She stumbled over a bulge in the water-stained parquet floor. Recovering her balance, she felt woozy, and her heart fluttered.

Paint chips were piled up in corners. Mold blackened the ceiling and the bare cracked walls. In the middle of the room, the wood frame of a Louis XV settee lay upside down.

George followed her into the room.

She said, "This is creepy. Isn't this the same room we saw from outside?"

She walked over to a pair of tall casement windows, their panes covered with green scum. Through the muck, she could barely discern a marble lion head.

Frowning she said, "That looks like the same fountain."

George put a protective arm around her waist, and guided her outside to the main entrance.

"Let's go back around again, so we can figure this out."

"Darling, I'm scared. It's something to do with the issues I'm sorting out with Dr. Sand. Too many abusive alcoholic ghosts rattling around in my family attic."

"Ghosts aren't real. I deal with the dead hands of testators every day. No matter how much the family fights over the will, the dead don't reappear."

Together they walked outside, around the side of the chateau. They approached the marble lion head. But now, dimly in view through a scum-encrusted window, was a dilapidated room with an overturned Louis XV settee. They glimpsed the vague figures of tourists through an open door on the far left. Indeed, there was that same woman with the red hair, chattering and gesticulating, her jewels flashing.

"This is impossible. I can't grasp it," she said.

"Let's ask the guide. There has to be a logical explanation." George squeezed her hand.

The two circled around to the front of the chateau. The Frenchwoman stood smoking a cigarette at the end of the terrace. George approached her.

"*Excusez-nous madame.* We were surprised earlier to see your living tableau in the billiard room. The model is very true to life."

She crushed the cigarette stub on the curly head of a putto carved on a stone urn.

"How do you say this? Tableau, to live? I do not understand."

"The actors who dress up in period costumes to show the tourists. That girl decked out as the queen, in that beautiful eighteenth-century dress, we were very taken with her."

"Ah, a *tableau vivant*? *Mon dieu, non, c'est ridicule.* We would never turn our precious heritage into that kind of Disneyland vulgar display."

"Has the refurbishing of the chateau started yet?"

"*Non, non, monsieur*, did you not pay attention to my explanation? The chateau will be closed for restoration in the springtime."

Karen and George glanced at one another. Karen mumbled a merci, and then bolted, sprinting on a gravel path that wound away from the chateau, toward the park. George followed at a deliberate pace, scrunching his face, working out the puzzle. How could such bizarre data form a logical pattern?

Out of breath, Karen plopped down on a stone bench

near a marble statue of a naked sea nymph. He caught up a minute later and sat beside her.

She spoke first, her voice trembling.

"I believe in evil spirits. I wish I didn't. My family ghosts destroy everything good in my life. Just wait, they'll drive you away from me."

She watched a red squirrel scrambling down the trunk of a plane tree.

He said, "Religion, a so-called spiritual world—it's all made up to frighten us as children, to gain control of our minds. Rational adults grow out of all this silly stuff and think for themselves."

She said, "If not a ghost, then what?"

The squirrel now darted up the torso of the sea nymph, pausing to nibble her right breast.

He chuckled. "An adroit move by that clever flaneur rodent."

"Be serious, George."

He returned to the question. "Physicists might answer that there is a time warp in that billiard room. Einstein proved mathematically that time warps are possible. The queen sits reading in 1789, let's say on the day before the royal family finally flees. She knows that an ominous rabble has gathered at the gates, and retires to read and reflect in a secret place, a billiard room where nobody would think to search for her, uniformed guards nearby. She concludes that all is lost. The moment is fraught with psychic energy, and falls out of ordinary time. Therefore, the queen is constantly fading in and out, and visible to strangers in their own time."

She said, "There are more things in this world than are dreamt of in math equations. Or, for that matter, in the all the cases in your law books. I'm not going to bring this up with Dr. Sand. He already thinks I'm loopy."

CURIOUS AFFAIRS

He bussed her on the cheek. "Well, the whole point of Paris is adventure and romance. This day has certainly been adventuresome. So let's concentrate on romance. No worries, sweetheart. It's all to the good. It will never be bad between us."

They rose from the bench and walked arm-in-arm on the lanes that wound through the park, past the palace, and out the front gates to the train station. It was four o'clock, and the car was half empty. Once the train settled into its steady rocking rhythm, George dozed, his head pillowed against Karen's arm. She sat upright and alert, watching out the window as an Impressionist landscape unfolded, the fields dotted with cattle and bordered by rows of fifty-foot poplar trees, their green foliage dusted with autumnal yellow. She longed for this whirlwind amour to solidify into a permanent attachment, marriage, a home together. Here, at long last, was her chance for a stable, loving relationship with a sane and sensible man. It was crucial to project feminine serenity, or else he would retreat. She vowed to continue her talks with Dr. Sand, who would help her exorcise those demons that haunted her. Most important, she must avoid any future entanglements with the uncanny.

She would suggest they spend tomorrow morning together in the Louvre. The Blue Guide described in detail the floor plans and the masterpieces that hung on its walls. No untoward surprises were possible in those well-mapped, tourist-clogged rooms. She would make sure they did not stray into musty side corridors, the uncatalogued jumble of Egyptian antiquities stolen by Napoleon, where only the great god Ptah knew how many vindictive mummies hurled curses at unsuspecting museum-goers.

Recovery

I AM AT LOOSE ENDS the first Saturday morning after my brother Charles checks into a thirty-day rehab program in Novato, thirty miles north of San Francisco. This is his second go-round. He relapsed about two years ago, after his celebration of six years sobriety with a cake at Alcoholics Anonymous. This whole mess started, it must have been in college, those chugging contests with his fraternity brothers, the pep pills for all-nighters before exams. I've been teased my whole life for my goody two-shoes teetotalism. I'm his forty-year-old sister, younger than he by five years, old enough to be stoic about it all. There are only the two of us, and we are both never-married—that by itself might be a red flag for some kind of dysfunction.

We are transplants to the Bay Area. Charles encouraged me to move for the excitement, the cultural life. He was a superstar, went to Stanford, has a lucrative career as an investment banker. I'm quite in his shadow, a graduate of a small women's college nobody ever heard of. I'm a client service associate at a downtown brokerage firm, Charles found me the job, and I manage to support myself, but there's no money left over for glitz. I believe he's ashamed of me, that I don't measure up. Still, I might have been closer to him, more sisterly, more helpful and loving, but how exactly, I don't know.

I simply don't care this morning how I look. I throw

on faded mommy-jeans and scrunch back my hair into a scraggly ponytail. I climb the mile-long slope that rises from my Cow Hollow apartment to Russian Hill, a gentrified block, a Peet's coffee shop across the street from a boulangerie, outside both places, long lines of fit urbanites in trendy sneakers, staring at their phones and texting, compulsively twitching their thumbs. These crowded glamorous places make me nervous, and so I turn the other way, deliberately seeking solitude.

After a few blocks, the tone of the street is grittier, a liquor store wedged between a pawnshop and a sex-toys emporium, cigarette butts and beer bottles littering the gutter. Ignoring caution, I turn into a narrow alleyway, unmarked with any sign, street of no return, perhaps?—if the begrimed asphalt could speak. About halfway down its murky length is a bookshop, the display windows stuffed to the gills, a cart of bargain books outside, almost completely blocking the pavement. The sign over the door reads: *Welcome. We feature soulful and scholarly books from the world's spiritual traditions.* I certainly am in a soul-searching phase, and I value scholarship.

I push open the heavyweight door. A wind-chime tinkles. The air smells of book glue mingled with lavender and cloves over a base note of mildew. The ceilings are high, higher than the room is wide, so that the space seems topsy-turvy, as if beached on its side by some crazed architect. Bookshelves line the walls from the dark plank floor to the ceiling frescoed with an alchemical sun and zodiac stars.

A clerk dressed in a flowered cotton peasant dress sits reading a book on a cushioned barstool behind a vintage brass National cash register. In the dim light I can't make out her features, except for gray hair wisping around a thin wrinkled face and tumbling in a disheveled mass down to an undefined waist. I'm in no mood to make eye contact, so I push past her to the back of the shop. The shelves have parchment labels written in black ink in a cursive script—Astrology, Hermetic Paths—ah, here's one that might help me: *Recovery*.

I sit on a kickstool, and begin examining the books on the lower shelves, removing them one by one. All have glossy covers and photos of smiling, tanned authors with too-white teeth, and most are printed on acid-free paper that could last a lifetime, and this makes me suspicious. If the book is any good, wouldn't a confident publisher use cheap paper, assuming that the reader will recover immediately and no longer require its advice? And who's paying for all that dental work anyway? I crane my neck to decipher titles on the higher shelves. I lose track of how much time elapses, but finding myself once again near the cash register, I realize that the clerk is watching me.

She blinks once through owlish tortoise-shell spectacles. "Welcome." The voice is gravelly like that of a long-term smoker. "How can I assist?"

I mumble that I'm just browsing.

"Ah, we have many such as you. Do you seek any specific wisdom?"

This inquiry should startle me, but it doesn't really. My year in Al-Anon has accustomed me to odd abrupt questions. That's another thing that I'm upset about. Al-Anon is the twelve-step program for families of alcoholics. While the rambunctious alcoholics are yukking it up in AA meetings in vast high school gyms, their disheartened loved ones are huddled together like the early Christians hiding from the Romans, in covert bare rooms in church basements. I'm the plodding dutiful one, and have attended Al-Anon faithfully while the brilliant, irrepressible Charles blows off AA. Of course, you can't change the way "they" are. It's like asking a skunk to please not stink.

I muster a noncommittal reply. "No, nothing in particular. I take anything that's on offer, any wisdom, that is."

I now realize that there is something strange about this woman, over and above her diction, the formal and not-quite-grounded language that Benedictine monks and Orthodox rabbis and Hindu gurus use. She is maybe not a female, and perhaps, not even a human. As I study her, I realize that a woman-sized blue gecko is talking to me, a book clasped in the webbing of its forelegs. Its scaly skin shimmers with the tiniest hint of iridescence. This should alarm me, but the ambience of this curious place has relaxed my guard. Anything seems possible. I glance at the cover, trying not to appear too nosy. Something about Paracelsus.

"I believe we have encountered one another before?" The lizardly mouth gapes open and shut while contemplating me.

"No, I don't think so. People always ask me that. They fill in my nondescript features with their own inventions, like they're drawing me on an etch-a-sketch."

"Ah, perhaps from another lifetime then. Your energy seems familiar."

"Meaning what, exactly?" I hope my tone has not turned too edgy or impolite. I try so very hard not to judge others, and to be nice to minimum-wage workers.

"There is an indigo aura around you. You are an old soul, on a spiritual path."

"I doubt that. Though I did read Shirley MacLaine twenty years ago. And I love to wander into Catholic churches in the off-hours, when nobody else is there."

"May I ask where you are from?"

"Nowhere in particular. Our family moved around a lot. We lived in better new-built suburbs everywhere."

"Ah, a woman with wings."

"Mostly a woman with a boring childhood. There was no there, there. Anywhere."

"And now?"

"Same old. Commute, work, sleep. Pretty boring. And lonely. It feels likes there's no real me anywhere in there."

Geez, I thought, this is turning into a therapy session. Wonder what the price is. Speaking of prices, it's a lucky break that Charles's first-class medical insurance covers the cost of rehab. He chose an upscale "executive" place. The patients scribble their angst in fancy leather journals and there's a pasture somewhere nearby where they can pet horses.

"You lingered in our Recovery section. For what reason? You do not manifest signs of addiction."

I stare at the lizard. Why I answer, I cannot say, except that I am desperate to talk to someone, anyone. I decide it must be female, otherwise why would it wear a dress? And she seems safe, an introverted reptilian type who won't criticize or gossip.

"My brother's cross-addicted to alcohol and amphetamines, and he's checked into rehab, his second try. I'm trying to recover also, from what, I'm not sure, maybe from idolizing him all these years, only to realize he's an out-of-control wreck."

Sometimes I fight back tears when I talk about Charles. But this morning, I'm numb. The gecko's tail flicks ever so slightly. Does that mean she sympathizes?

I add a random comment. "He's older, and I always wanted to be just like him. Now what? My pedestal needs a hero."

"Do you meditate?" she says.

Why the change of subject? But actually I'm grateful that she's not interested in the soap-opera of Charles's erratic behavior.

"Oh, no. Too restless."

She says, "Have you ever been properly instructed in meditation techniques?"

Why is she so interested in meditation? Lizards have low metabolisms, and love to bask for hours in the sun. Maybe meditating helps when hawks are circling overhead.

I plunge into my anecdote about meditation, the one that I've polished in Al-Anon, about the silent Buddhist retreat in Napa seven years ago. No food, only vegetable broth and carrot sticks that you were supposed to eat slowly with mindfulness. I went to the dojo sessions the first day, and then quit. Every morning I walked to a nearby mom and pop café for a full country breakfast, fried eggs and pancakes and bacon, and took afternoon naps, and holed up in my room, reading.

"Reading what?" she says.

Oh dear. In Al-Anon nobody ever asks me this question. I'm secretive about my books. But I forge ahead. After all, we're in a bookshop. "I read a lot of literature. It was my year of reading Proust. During that whole week, I was absorbed in *Swann's Way*. The landscape could have been Combray. The eucalyptus trees grew straight like poplars, and the crape myrtles were in full blossom, like hawthorn."

"Were you alone?"

This creature has mesmerized me into an earnest, somewhat addled, self-revelatory trance. I reply honestly, if mechanically.

"No, my then-boyfriend talked me into going. Later he dumped me. He complained that my chakras were in disarray, that my animus was over-inflated, that dating me was way too much work."

"And since then?"

"I've only been with two other men, both secular types,

who loved sports and hated books. They sabotaged my reading. Mostly I've been alone."

Why I am telling her all this stuff? I thought. There's a boundary issue here somewhere.

"Ever with a woman?" she says.

I stare at her. Uh oh.

"No, I've never, I mean, some of my good friends are lesbians, but they do their thing, whatever that thing is, I'm not even sure, I mean I don't do anything with them. Not that I do anything with anybody."

"I recommend that you study the spiritual causation of addiction," she says.

"You mean the twelve-step stuff? I've been a regular in Al-Anon every Wednesday night for the past year, my brother's therapist recommended it."

I pause, and then I confess my halfhearted involvement. "I don't have a sponsor, so I'm not getting the most I can out of it, they keep saying that we co-dependents are sicker than our alcoholics, that I need to work the steps."

In point of fact, Al-Anon has begun to get on my nerves. It seems a kind of truth-or-dare game, and there's a weird competitive vibe: my alcoholic is crazier than your alcoholic-addict. So much weeping, and that creepy box of Kleenex set aggressively in the middle of the circle. And those inane slogans. *There are no mistakes, only lessons. Keep coming back, it works if you work it.* What nonsense. The light at the end of the tunnel, another train.

The lizard puts down Paracelsus and adjusts her spectacles. She stares directly into my eyes. I'm nettled, but I don't flinch.

"Those twelve steps work on a superficial level, but to discover the source of addiction, you must excavate a channel down into the primal deep. A malignant archon infected your brother with negative dark energy when he was a fetus floating in your mother's womb."

I say nothing, but my expression must be puzzled. What is she talking about?

"We keep the esoteric literature in the celestial heights, out of reach of our casual visitors," she says.

She gestures with saurian toes toward a rickety wooden library ladder, its metal wheels nestled in a metal track that runs along a mid-level shelf.

"I invite you to climb Jacob's ladder to peruse these texts. I will position it for you."

The metal track squeaks as she slides the ladder from ten feet away, and centers it. She points upward.

"You see, up there, on the ninth level of shelves."

My practical gut screams: No way. But a vapory presentiment urges me on. I step on the bottom rung and start to climb. The ladder sways and wobbles. The volumes hover above me, beckoning. I scan the shelves, left to right. Dusty paperbacks sit cheek by jowl with antique treatises bound in crumbling calfskin. A melange, and yet a careful intelligence has selected these volumes. My head is buzzing, about what exactly, I cannot articulate, a diffuse sense of well-being, that I am on the verge of—what? My common sense is howling: Jacob's ladder, what a crock. Get down and get the heck outta here, right now. The calm voice carries on, whispers: Pay no attention to that nattering naysayer. Stay, stay, you are safe here, there is healing wisdom in this place.

The Curious Affair
of Helen and Franz

At six o'clock on a June morning in the year of the Common Era 2005, Helen Bramer strolled on a paved fire road in the Santa Monica mountains of Los Angeles. IPod in hand, she listened to the Schubert G Minor sonata through lightweight earphones.

The cool dawn air was glorious, scented with eucalyptus and sage, and the Schubert airs were glorious. She hummed along to the lilting theme of the violin embellished by the arpeggios of the piano. The tempo of the music was faster in this, the final movement, and she flourished her right hand in figures-of-eight, as if conducting an orchestra.

Following the curvature of the hilltop, the fire road slanted left. A gnarled oak tree marked the summit of the hill. To the right of the tree, a path overgrown with brush meandered down the steep slope. Helen meant someday to strike out into that wilderness, but feared being scraped by burrs or bruised by stones, or worse, attacked by predators. Humans could only guess at the carnage wreaked by wild mythic creatures during those nights when fierce Santa Ana winds knocked over eucalyptus trees as tall as the masts of whaling ships. Even in calm broad daylight, coyotes trotted in pairs along the road. There were often mountain lion sightings. Once she had tiptoed around a limp rattlesnake snoozing in the warm afternoon sun.

On reaching the tree Helen turned off the iPod and removed the earphones. A gaggle of sparrows was warbling and cooing, and three crows cawed, fighting over some bit of avian turf. A slight breeze rustled the leaves of the oak, and its outer branches swayed and bowed. She surveyed the path, which was visible only halfway down the hillside, where it vanished, concealed by a marine fog layer enshrouding the canyon below.

A loud whistling caught her ear. The sound came from the mist roiling in the canyon. She recognized a lyrical happy-sad melody from celestial spheres: the fourth movement allegro theme of Schubert's G Major String Quartet, the four instruments in intimate conversation, familiar from when she was a little girl, every Sunday at her grandmother's Washington Park brick colonial for midday dinner, the Magnavox stereo cabinet and the collection of classical 33 LP's.

Better to avoid the whistler. On these morning walks she savored her solitude, brooding over Eric's perfidy of two years ago, over the x-rated e-mails to another woman. She still whimpered on her early morning walks, and wept late at night into her pillow. But she paused to listen, and admire the panorama before her, the hilltops a pointillist carpet of yellow broom punctuated by ten-foot high yucca stalks crowned with plumes the color of clotted cream, the ocean fog tinged sunrise-pink nestling in the canyon.

A plump young man dressed in an old-fashioned black wool morning coat and gray breeches suddenly emerged out of the fog. He bounded up the hill, thumping the ground with an alpenstock, a carved wooden walking stick that seemed familiar to her. Her family possessed a similar walking stick, an heirloom handed down over many generations. How odd. No movie was being shot in the area. She had seen no vans or camera crews. Of course, crazed homeless men wandered in these hills. She rejected this theory, as he was not filthy or wild-eyed like a drug-addled panhandler.

Now the young man stopped. The top of his head came just to her chin. He blinked out on the world through myopic eyes covered with thick spectacles, and his boyish face was framed with long unruly brown hair. His whistling broke off abruptly. Helen took up the musical line in her thin untrained alto. His impish lips turned downward and his brows furrowed. Then he spoke, and although the language seemed an old-fashioned German, she somehow caught his meaning.

"Gruss Gott, fraulein, and how do you know my melody already? I am only just composing it. Are you an angel muse, a goddess come to assist me? I have become lost in these mountains. Can you inform me the way to the lodgings of my friend Josef von Spaun? He expects me tonight."

He used the formal second person "you," polite, restrained. His features matched the picture in the Newbould biography of Franz Schubert that she had been reading last night and had tossed amidst a slew of books on her nightstand. She stepped toward him and touched the fabric of his coat. The weave felt similar to the moth-eaten wool serge coat that her father had saved from World War II, and which he still pulled out of the front hall closet to show visitors. The young man startled at her touch.

"Gott im Himmel, fraulein, but your uncourteous manners are singular. Did you not a proper education receive?"

His protest discomfited her, and her face flushed pink. "I'm sorry. But you can't possibly be who I think you are."

Glaring at her, he squared his shoulders and thrust out his chest. "Your curiosity about my identity yourself does not excuse. Even chambermaids fresh from the country do not poke and prod at a personage without permission."

"But if I'm a goddess wouldn't I be exempt from the rules of courtesy?"

"Ah, but a goddess would already know my identity, unless she were mayhap only a water sprite. But there is neither a river nor a lake nor even a brook in this vicinity."

Helen tried to concentrate on a logical response. The situation was baffling. Perhaps a friendly American hello would put them both at ease.

"My dear Franz—I may call you Franz, dear Herr Schubert—as a goddess may take liberties?"

He grimaced. But then he shrugged as if it were too much trouble to argue with her about her use of the informal "thou."

"So then, fraulein, you cannot direct me to the residence of Josef?"

"No, I don't know his house, that is, I don't know it actually, but I've read about it and seen a photograph. I didn't have time to visit it on my trip to Austria."

The young man seemed for the first time to examine his surroundings.

"This landscape is uncanny, is it not? The flora differs from the firs in the woods surrounding Vienna."

A scary idea suddenly crystallized, that he might have emerged from an Einstein-Rosen wormhole and that the entrance to some otherworld might be nearby. Yet another reason to panic in this desolate chaparral. She stammered out a reply.

"I don't know what to tell you, that is, if you are really a body, and not a spirit, then you must have lost your way. In fact, you have strayed somehow, I don't know how, to America, at the western edge, near the Pacific ocean, and it is, that is it was when I left my house a little while ago, the beginning of the twenty-first century. Unless, and this is possible, it's the other way round, and I've lost my way instead. Or, it could be a complete muddle, could both of us be lost?"

The young man frowned.

"Ah, so you tell me I am multiple leagues from Vienna and decades in advance of my proper time. Be that as it may, in point of fact you are a goddess, are you not, you can convey me back, no?"

"I haven't a clue as to how you can get back. Because, I'm only a too, too mortal woman, that's for sure, and completely ordinary, unlucky in love, though come to think of it, the goddess Aphrodite never found her heart's desire either, but never mind. And by the way, I haven't yet introduced myself, my name is Helen Bramer, but please call me Helen."

The young man's face brightened.

"Well then, fraulein, if you have a plump feather bed, and nourishing chicken broth, and excellent writing paper, I can compose just as easily in your house as in Josef's. And we will await an answer from God. Surely, He, Who transported me here, can return me. It is obvious that He has ordained an encounter with a beautiful woman to console and assist and inspire me."

Helen blushed at the compliment. She was, at her core, an insecure teenage girl, desperate to think that against all odds she might turn out to be pretty. And from the young Schubert himself, well, this was indeed a "moment musicale" to be treasured.

His voice now dropped to a whisper, and his eyes glanced upward toward the sky.

"God does not let me idle long. Compose I must, and constantly, lest the demons attack. Please, Fraulein Bramer, shelter me in your home, and God will succor me."

His self-invitation delighted her. Helen was not one to let strangers into her home. But midwestern common sense

116   CURIOUS AFFAIRS

did not apply to this unique situation. Her mind began its chatter. I'm not ready for a guest, especially one so distinguished. Where will he sleep, there aren't enough towels, suppose he trashes things? Suppose he has a special diet? Suppose he . . . the objections were unending.

❋

And so, Helen guided Herr Schubert the mile to her Spanish bungalow set back a little from the main road. They walked up the driveway framed on either side with four cypress trees. At the entrance she opened the heavy arched oak door and motioned him to step in first. He looked around for an urn to stash his alpenstock, but finding none, handed it to her.

Immediately he sprinted across the Persian carpet to the ebony Steinway grand piano gleaming in the far corner. Usually, visitors remarked on the gloss of the shellac, but showed no interest otherwise. She no longer played regularly and could not remember the last time the piano lid had been raised. The instrument had not been tuned in several years, and the flat pitch of its keys assuredly would prove embarrassing.

Herr Schubert opened the fallboard, sat, placed his chubby hands on the keyboard, and picked out a cheerful air. Humming, he then improvised an ebullient variation. His face beamed with unabashed pleasure.

"Ah, fraulein, in Vienna such divine instruments we do not possess. Although not a perfect pitch, still the sound is a delight fabricated by angels in the workshops of paradise. Only in my reveries have I encountered such dulcet tones."

A relief, he liked the instrument. Of course in the 1820's the technology of the grand piano had not yet been perfected. He now closed the fallboard, and stood up.

"I will be very happy here. And of what will my sleeping quarters consist?"

Helen had no ready answer. Should she offer Franz her bedroom? Twenty-five years ago she had inherited $600,000 from a great-aunt. When the surprise check arrived in the mail she had deposited it in her checking account. Within a year, every last dollar had been spent to buy this home and furnish it. She had created a "room of her own." The queen-sized bed was set in an ornate wrought iron frame. The mauve silk comforter was coordinated with chintz draperies splashed with blue and mauve parrots. Etchings of Scottish castles hung on the sponge-painted lavender walls. No, not even for a genius composer would she give up her sanctum.

She led him down a long hallway to a windowless room furnished with a pressboard desk and swivel chair, a desktop computer, a beige stainless steel filing cabinet, and a leather club chair. A Murphy bed was set into the far wall. She cleared her throat and fidgeted.

"This is my spare room. Had I realized that you would be visiting, Herr Schubert, I would have fixed it up better."

"Ah, but fraulein, this one is splendid. It will be as quiet as a grotto in a monastery. I will obtain the rest I require."

Thank goodness the room satisfied him.

She said, "Come to the kitchen, so I can fix you a nice breakfast."

Helen cooked oatmeal and toasted wheat bread. She brewed espresso, poured it into mugs, and dolloped a thick layer of whipped cream on top. The two sat at the butcher block table in her breakfast nook. Herr Schubert wolfed down the cereal and toast, scattering crumbs everywhere and spattering globs of strawberry preserves on the table and the floor. It was obvious he would be a lot of trouble.

She picked up her BlackBerry and speed-dialed her assistant's voicemail. Speaking rapidly, she stated she was sick, and would not be in the office today. Schubert seemed fascinated by her actions.

"Fraulein, what is that contraption, and to whom are you speaking about your ailments? You appear to be hale and hearty."

"This is a machine we use nowadays. My words are being recorded. You see, we don't actually have to talk to anyone. And being sick is the standard excuse for not showing up at work."

"Be that as it may, you appear as wealthy as a countess. How is it that you labor as if you were a charwoman?"

"It's too difficult to explain. All I can say is that the better off we are, the more we work."

She settled him at the piano, and brought him blank copy paper and three sharpened number two pencils. Back in the kitchen, she loaded the dishes into the dishwasher and wiped up the mess. Like having a toddler, but worth it, as every mother said.

She walked into the living room. "Be back soon, I'll buy some paper for you," she said. How could a prodigy compose his masterworks on flimsy twenty-pound copy paper?

Franz barely glanced up as she prepared to leave. Picking up the car keys she left him hunched over the piano, tinkering with a pleasant tune that seemed to ramble through a magical forest, leap like a trout in a mountain stream, rest on top of a mist shrouded mountain.

❊

She drove the fifteen miles on the backed-up freeway and clogged streets to a music supply shop. Thirty years ago, she used to buy classical scores there, when she had briefly resumed her piano lessons. At that time she had rented a spinet in her cramped apartment near the La Brea Tar Pits. As a child she had been a star piano student, entered by her teacher in several statewide competitions, but she had abandoned serious practice at the age of fourteen, when her academic classes became too demanding. The Steinway now stood as a silent reminder of a talent she had let lapse.

Would Franz be there when she returned? This was a fool's errand, a waste of time and money. Of course the apparition could not be real, and would disappear, poof! just as it had appeared. What would she do with blank composition paper? The private high school near her had a stellar music department, and would appreciate a donation.

Since the breakup of her three-year relationship with Eric, weeds of glum pessimism had strangled the secret garden of her imagination. Her walks, her reveries, her love for books and chamber music, none of these rejuvenated her. She had stood firm in the belief that men and women shouldn't live together outside marriage. Living in sin, it was called during her growing up years. Eric was not the first man who had become exasperated when she refused to cohabit. All too soon she had reached her mid-fifties, unmarried and childless, and was sinking into a kind of melancholia, regretting the roads not taken.

Her goddaughter Emily's wedding last month was a shock. Was it already twenty-six years ago that she had held tight to the wriggling baby who squalled while the elderly priest mumbled the Latin blessings and sprinkled holy water? She had sat in a cluster of cousins at the reception, held in the Cross Creek Country Club in Springfield, Illinois, introduced as the Hollywood aunt. How did she remain so thin—perhaps nibbled only on lettuce leaves, a high metabolism, like a rabbit? Where was her husband, and how many children did she have? They raised myriad eyebrows, some from the Illinois side of the family, thin and once reddish blonde now a faded gray, the others from the Kentucky side, thick and once black, now salt and pepper.

Her hairdresser Max ensured that her hair was shoulder length, professionally tousled, and Clairol blonded. She passed for forty. But there it was, the reality of getting older, alone. Her younger colleagues seemed to show disrespect; they sensed she was road-kill in the new economy marketplace. She felt passed over, not a part of, estranged from the normalcy of family bonds. Where was she to find a little love in this cruel world? Thank God she had accumulated a portfolio of blue chip stocks and bonds to keep her aging body and her drooping soul together.

It took her the usual ten minutes to find a parking space on a side street. She fed quarters into a parking meter, walked two blocks to the music shop, and entered its musty gloom. Door chimes tinkled. Musical instruments and sheet music cluttered the room from the dirt-crusted linoleum floor to the water-stained acoustic tile ceiling. She scooped up a tall stack of high quality twelve-stave music manuscript paper. The bill was seventy dollars. The clerk, whose freckled face was topped with frizzy red hair, stared at her.

"I've seen you somewhere. Are you a composer of film scores? Or perhaps a professor at USC Thornton?"

She was uncertain how to reply. She could hardly tell him the truth.

"Oh no, it's for a friend. He is a young composer. Some day he'll be a household name, but as of yet, well, you know how the world treats its geniuses."

He nodded his agreement. "Do I ever. I got a PhD in musicology at twenty-five but here I am, at forty-five, living pillar to post. The Web is wiping out our business. At least I occasionally meet a gorgeous woman."

She did not pursue this flirtation. Smiling at him she left the store.

A three car collision slowed the freeway to stop and go. When she turned into her driveway two hours later, she saw her neighbor Roxanne out for a walk, watching her gray, pink-beribboned Yorkshire terrier spin around in circles preparing to lift its teensy leg. Roxanne's dry-cleaned skinny jeans encased a tight derriere. Unpleasant, these Botoxed women who knew the cost of everything and the value of nothing. Roxanne waved, but Helen pretended not to see her, pulled into the garage, and pushed the button to close the door.

Franz was still bent over the piano. He hadn't disappeared! She laid the stack of paper on an end table. Finally he noticed her, and then when he spotted the paper, jumped up and seized a dozen sheets.

"Ah fraulein, this is perfection, how can I ever show you proper gratitude?"

"I'm sorry about the pencils. I'll buy you a proper fountain pen tomorrow," she said.

"Heaven, this is." He waggled his index finger toward her. "And this one, she is my own empyrean muse."

❄

That evening, Helen roasted chicken and prepared several rice and vegetable dishes, puzzling over complex directions in her Julia Child cookbook. For the first time since her breakup, she set the Queen Anne cherry table in the dining room with a white linen cloth, and lit two white taper candles in silver candelabra. Her Rosenthal china gleamed in the flickering shadows cast by an antique French chandelier resplendent with gilt-leaf cherubs.

"Ah, fraulein, this is magnificent. Let us toast my swift and safe return."

They clinked Waterford crystal goblets filled with Stag's Leap cabernet. Eric had left a dozen bottles of wine and several fifths of rare single malt Scotches in her kitchen cabinet. Until now, she had not opened even one bottle. He was a hard-driving commercial real estate broker, and a connoisseur of wine and liquor. His irritation with her disinterest in fine spirits and her dislike of his drinking had been a source of tension.

Within a few days Helen and Franz settled into a domestic routine. Both awoke at five-thirty, and walked together on the fire road. She fixed breakfast, either oatmeal or eggs, with toast or croissants and fruit. She scurried off in frantic haste to her job. He remained behind, holed up for hours in the plain spare room. Occasionally he went to the piano to experiment with a melody. He was short-sighted, perpetually in a brown study, oblivious to his surroundings, constantly muttering and singing to himself, and jotting down notes. He never asked about the microwave, the electric lights, the computer, the Acura parked in her garage, the occasional automobile that whizzed by.

❄

The hot smog of July settled into the canyons. Crows squabbled, wasps buzzed, crickets trilled. At night, coyotes howled as they cornered defenseless creatures who shrieked when death fangs grabbed their throats.

Helen lingered over breakfast, drove in much later to work, and left much earlier. Her reputation at the office began to deteriorate, as her in-box piled up. At home, she dressed in silk pajamas instead of her habitual mommy jeans and tees. She appeared always made up with powder and mascara, and with hair set in loose curls. She shopped and cooked for dear Franz, washed his clothes, collected and organized the musical fragments into bound notebooks. Every night she pulled out and made up the Murphy bed, and every morning she placed the bed back and tidied up the room.

Never mind the extra expense and the fact that her whole world was now topsy-turvy and her job might be in jeopardy. She had never put so much effort into performing wifely tasks. A delicious fantasy preoccupied her. Franz had always been with her, even from the time of her childhood spent in an attic room with faded wallpaper covered with yellow roses. The chimes in the belfry of the Gothic parish church tolled out vespers in the summer evenings. In those days, she had read *Half Magic*, a story of children who found imperial Roman coins that when rubbed, transported them to other times. She hoped that even one of the silver dimes she placed so carefully in the slits of her coin collector folio would turn out to be ancient, and magical. But never had any magic manifested in her life.

About ten years ago, she'd investigated Kabbalah, the genuine thing, not the red-string celebrity hype. Her friend Esther had brought her as a guest to a study group led by Rebbe Menachem Mendel. On ten Tuesday nights she had sat, intimidated and silent, on a folding chair in a bare room in a minuscule orthodox shul in the Fairfax district. The rebbe instructed a class of fourteen in the concept of the transmigration of souls, and in the mystic secrets of the great Kabbalist Isaac Luria of Safed. Her sober adult self half-believed these speculations. Any Lurianist would shrug off Franz's appearance as routine. Magical, no—simply a manifestation of the complex processes of tikkun, the repair of the world.

She and Esther were still in contact and met several times a year for coffee. They had not discussed Kabbalah in a long time. Should she call her? Better to say nothing to anyone, at least not yet.

She was not sure, really, if Franz were real. But he must be real. He ate the real food she served him, and wore the real blue jeans and jumbo size Hanes T-shirts she bought for him. Before her eyes, he was composing, with a real Visconti fountain pen, on tangible paper, a song cycle, the *Winterreisse.*

One Sunday morning, Helen tiptoed outside to retrieve the *Los Angeles Times* lying in a puddle in the driveway. The gardener must have knocked a sprinkler head out of alignment. Irritated, she picked up the sopping wet plastic wrap and turned it over. Water streamed onto the asphalt.

"Hello, darling, who is your visitor?"

She looked up. Roxanne held the Yorkshire, stroking its silky hair with long red acrylic fingernails.

There was no avoiding some kind of pleasantry.

"That's Cousin Franz from Vienna. That whole side of the family never came to America. I guess they're checking us out now."

Roxanne's waxed eyebrows arched. "Oh? Well, he seems like a peculiar sort. What does he do?"

"He's brilliant, a world-class scholar. He has a doctorate in Renaissance musicology, and decided to take the summer off before he goes back to his professorship in Vienna."

Roxanne put the dog down, holding on to a bright pink leash studded with rhinestones.

"Well, my dear, don't support him for too long. But, you know how we women are, forever taking in strays."

Helen shrugged. "Perhaps you're right. You know, Roxanne, some delights in life are just very expensive."

Roxanne smirked. "Cheaper to hire it by the hour, darling."

It was impossible to fake civility. Scowling Helen turned abruptly and walked inside.

That afternoon, Helen scoured the Newbould biography, hunting for clues as to her own existence. Was she inspiring him? The Unknown Lady of the Song Cycle. It was thrilling to think of her mysterious and important place in musical history. Did he desire her? Would he be her lover? More than once, the moonlight streaming through her windows woke her as she reached for him, certain in her sleepy delusion that he was caressing her. But he never approached her. He never shared any insights, never requested an introduction to other people. She had so hoped (and dreaded, for what explanation would she give the guests?) he would allow her to act as hostess for one of those Schubertiade soirees that were the stuff of musical legend, but he never alluded to them.

In early August she turned down an out-of-town business trip. She sat across from her boss in his corner office. His brown eyes narrowed. He was a lean forty, his face impassive, a cobra, ready to strike.

"What is this, a refusal? We need you to go. You have been slacking off. Don't think management hasn't noticed."

"I can't travel anymore. I have an emergency at home. A cousin of mine is sick and needs my help."

She gazed into the middle distance, avoiding his eyes. The company encouraged "work/life balance" for the higher-ups, but not for lower level managers. Retribution would be slow but certain, an agonizing process of demotion and eventual firing. But she no longer cared about her work. All that mattered was that Franz was happy.

❋

One morning in early August, Franz did not appear at the habitual time. Baffled, she waited a quarter hour, and then walked alone on the usual path. On her return, she folded mushrooms into an omelet and popped English muffins into the toaster. Franz slouched into the kitchen, glared at the food, gulped down two cups of coffee, and disappeared. A door slammed. That evening, he hardly touched the prime rib. By ten o'clock, an empty fifth of single malt Scotch lay on its side near the Steinway.

Two weeks went by. He rarely spoke to her. Several bags of Oreo cookies disappeared every day. He demanded that she buy alcoholic beverages. The garbage can set out every Tuesday was piled high with empty beer cans and whiskey bottles. He slept an increasing number of hours. The air around him stank of stale sweat. His eyes were puffy and glazed over. He hummed less, and barely scribbled any notes on the composition paper. Whenever she attempted to converse, he simply looked past her, mumbling unintelligibly.

Helen now walked alone every morning. Every night, she clenched her pillow, gulping air into her lungs, her chest convulsing. Oh, the ingrate!

One Sunday, she met Esther at the Coffee Bean in Brentwood. They hugged, ordered double lattes, and sat down at a table. Rock music pulsated from overhead speakers and made talk difficult.

Esther said, "What's doing?"

Should Helen mention Franz? Her reply was noncommittal. "Same-old, same-old, work as usual, no man in my life. I think I've already had my last chance."

Esther showed off a three-carat engagement ring. "He's perfect in every way. I finally went to a matchmaker. Genuine Jewish shadchan. Why I didn't years ago, I can't believe, it's this heartless horrible city that makes it impossible to meet anyone."

Happy news, Helen was glad for her friend, wasn't she?

What was this twinge of envy? She asserted the conventional opinion: "We're all in our little isolated boxes. And the available men are spoiled egomaniacs. The good ones are taken."

Esther nodded. "Don't give up. There's someone out there for you. I'm telling you, get yourself a good go-between, an expert with a proven record."

Here was an opportunity for Helen to share her secret, to ask for advice. She hesitated. This crowded place seemed inappropriate. Many glamorous neurotics spilled unseemly details in public, and these revelations always made her wince.

She broached the subject offhandedly. "Remember our class together, with Reb Mendel, back in the day?"

Esther said, "He's a fantastic man. I've never made the full turn to orthodoxy, so I haven't seen him in an age."

"What do you think of transmigration of souls? And time travel, I always wondered what Kabbalah has to say."

Esther shrugged. "I gave all that stuff up. It's way too strange. I'm better off down in the here-and-now, thinking about the concrete." She pointed again to her ring. "Match-maker make me a match. Mine is very grounded in the everyday, and that's why she gets results."

Helen retreated. No sense in plunging any deeper. The reality was, she had nobody to whom she could reveal her situation. The talk turned to safe gossipy matters, their jobs, movies and books, Esther's recent trip to Israel.

❄

On a Saturday afternoon in late August, Helen sat propped against the oversized pillows on her bed, reading *The New Yorker* and sipping lemonade. The sound of water whooshing in the wall pipes alerted her that the shower was running. At long last, was Franz snapping out of his funk?

A little later, she sensed a presence. She looked out the French casement window. Sometimes curious deer sniffed at the glass. Nothing moved outside except a lizard scampering on the patio. She glanced toward the bedroom doorway. Her heart fluttered as she lay the magazine down. Franz lounged against the wall, hair glistening wet from his shower. He had never entered her snuggery. He walked over and sat on the edge of the bed.

"Fraulein," he declared, sweeping his chubby fingers toward the cypress and olive trees visible from her windows. "I have so wanted to see the Umbrian landscapes that the Florentine masters painted as backdrops for their Madonnas, and this must be very like. Wonderful, but," he added in a soft, choking voice, "I miss the woods of Vienna."

His next words sounded a death knell.

"You have been so very kind, and this is a magnificent house. And you are a gracious companion and a lovely woman. But, I want to see my friends."

Now his mouth was puckering and he was sobbing.

"I am terrified, because the melodies are receding. I cannot hear them clearly anymore. I fear the worst, that I am losing my gift. You must assist me. I must return."

She took his rotund face between her hands, and felt the fuzzy damp cheeks.

"My dearest love, you are a marvel and a genius. I want only the best for you."

Tears welled in her eyes. She grabbed his wrist and pulled him toward her. "Franz, my love, my dearest, come to bed. I will make you happy, happier than any man in any time, in any place." She kissed him full on his mouth.

His body froze and he pulled away from her.

"Fraulein, I must return. You misunderstand. It is life and death."

She found herself screaming at him. "What makes you

think I can help you? I told you from the beginning, I don't have any powers. You're the one who got lost. I never got lost, and if I did get lost, I would figure it out by myself. How can you expect me to know what to do?"

Turning on his heel, he stomped out of the room.

❊

Toxic shame, as slimy as black swamp mud, oozed into her psyche. Was she holding Franz against his will? But such a thought was ridiculous. How could she free him? She knew nothing of the ars magica, of the mechanics of vanishing and reappearing, of the re-shuffling of the time/space continuum deck of cards.

At six o' clock she knocked on the door of the little room.

"Go away, leave me in solitude."

"But my dearest, you must eat. Please come out."

"No, I am not hungry. Leave me, do not disturb me."

She went to bed at nine o'clock and cried herself to sleep. At four in the morning, she jolted awake. A full moon lit up her bedroom with a shimmering white light. She had been dreaming that Rebbe Mendel sat next to her, absorbed in a book, on a train traveling she knew not where. She lay awake, while the night melted into a warm sunny morning.

At breakfast, there was no sign of Franz. She knocked on his door. Silence.

At noon, she telephoned the shul. The rebbe answered.

Her hands were shaking. She mustered a businesslike tone.

"Of course, you probably don't remember me. I studied with you a few years ago, I'm not Jewish, I admit, my friend Esther brought me. I desperately need your help."

The baritone voice was gentle, encouraging. "There is a wedding today at five o'clock. But I can counsel you briefly at three."

The official annals of her family recorded no Jewish connections. Of course, there was that suspicious nineteenth-century peddler on her paternal German side, and she could never keep the math straight as to what negligible percentage of Jewish blood that might be. She dressed in faux orthodox garb, long rayon black skirt, white cotton long-sleeved blouse, gray beret, and black Mary Janes.

The shul was a small brick building. Hebrew letters were blazoned in gold leaf across the lintel of the large oak and iron door. The rebbe greeted her with a friendly nod. The holy man seemed timeless, a part of the warp and woof of the Jewish fabric, which, she always imagined, circled and wrapped the world in centuries-old wisdom.

They sat in the bare room on beige metal folding chairs, six feet across from one another. Near the doorway stood a slim youth, his black forelocks grazing his shoulders. In a monotone she stated the facts as she watched the rebbe's face.

"I need help with an impossible situation. The musical genius, Franz Schubert, you know of him?"

The rebbe pursed his lips, but said nothing.

"He was born in 1797 and died young in 1828. Somehow, at age twenty-nine, and at the height of his powers, he has gotten lost inside his own head. He turned up on a hiking path in the hills near my home. He has been staying with me for two months. He is desperate to return to his proper earthly plane."

The old man listened. He stroked his white beard that cascaded over his frayed black gabardine wool coat. He closed his eyes while rocking slightly back and forth, as if davening. His head seemed to sink into his frail thin body. Her short recital finished, she sighed, and slumped in her chair. The late afternoon sun slanted through a window near the ceiling, lighting up motes of dust. It seemed a minor eternity before he opened his black eyes. He spoke in a rasping whisper.

"My dear, this situation is more common than you might think. The average person sleepwalks through life. If he is poor, he longs to be rich. If he is rich, he seeks power. He does not study, he does not pursue the way of Torah. Therefore, he does not realize all the wondrous phenomena around him."

He cleared his throat.

"The sages report many such cases. I myself have experienced four in my lifetime. And it is my pleasure to assist you."

Helen straightened her shoulders. She had come to the right place. The rebbe leaned slightly forward.

"You yourself have caused this quandary through the intensity of your improper longings. You must understand that Hashem responds to our spiritual yearnings, often in ways that are extraordinary."

She studied the pattern of the vinyl floor. How did he know of her bitter isolation, of her romantic fancies?

"In the early morning just at daybreak, when the sun rises in the east, take your young genius back down the path on which he arrived. At the borderland where the fog meets the sun, hold his hand, and hand him the box that I will give you. Inside I will place a parchment scroll with a berakhah, a blessing transcribed especially for you. A messenger of Hashem will meet him, and transport him back to his proper place and time. The world will receive the gift of his lyrical melodies that will delight generations. And you, my dear, will receive a gift of wisdom. You will know

CURIOUS AFFAIRS

that all things are in harmony with the Power, Blessed Be He, Who orders the universe."

With a mischievous smile, he changed topics.

"And when are you planning to marry? It is more than enough time, my dear."

Helen knitted her brow. A flicker of anxiety passed over her face, but recollecting herself, she managed a self-conscious simper.

"Oh, I think Hashem has forgotten me. But I'll pray about it tomorrow, after I've solved this problem."

The rebbe disappeared into another room with the boy. Helen stood up and paced, circling the two chairs, and then she sat down and fidgeted with the buttons on her blouse. She trusted this man of God. Yet of course her logical mind was skeptical. Her work colleagues would snicker and her family would groan with disapproval were they to know.

She removed her checkbook and a ballpoint pen from her shoulder bag. As if guided by an automatic hand, her pen wrote the amount $540, which represented Franz's age on his next birthday multiplied by the number eighteen, the mystical number of life.

A long quarter hour passed. Reb Mendel returned through the doorway. She rose from the chair. He held a pocket-size metal box in his hands. The boy stood mute beside him.

"And here you are, my dear."

He placed the box on a wood table just inside the door. She mumbled a thank you, and set the check down on the table. He bowed, and replied in a Hebrew phrase that she did not understand.

When she returned, there was still no sign of Franz. Helen tucked the box underneath her panties in a dresser drawer scented with a rosewater sachet. He appeared briefly at dinnertime, and wolfed down bratwurst and kraut she had bought especially to charm him. Then he disappeared again.

The rebbe had pricked her conscience. She knew his instructions must be obeyed. But she decided to wait just a little while longer. Perhaps Franz yet would fall in love and beg to remain with her.

❄

In the following week, Helen redoubled her efforts to woo Franz. Every night, she prepared elaborate formal dinners. A Wonderbra emphasized her breasts under a black lacy camisole. He remained distant and sullen.

What was she to do? She choked back tears of pique. She would have to suffer, as much as a doomed soprano in a tragic opera, and let him go.

On Saturday just at dusk, she addressed him as they sat at dinner.

"Franz, my dearest, I have good news for you."

He barely glanced in her direction. He was staring out the window, watching a buck nibble on her pansy bed. He tapped a fork against the plate and glowered.

"I have obtained a magic spell that will send you back to Vienna at sunrise tomorrow. You will arrive within seconds of the time that you left."

Franz jumped up, knocking over the chair. He yodeled and then he hugged her, planting a sloppy kiss on her lips.

"My dear Helen, das ist herrlich! However can I express my gratitude? I will dedicate my next piano trio to you. I will never forget you."

He had never before used her first name.

"No, my love, the magic formula does not permit you to remember. Nor will you recall the music you've written here in this place. But we needed each other just for a little while. And I'm grateful."

He righted his chair, sat down, and stabbed at his steak.

"Ah, Helen, you are so good to me." He was talking now with a mouth full of the juicy pink meat. "You must of course keep my alpenstock."

After cleaning the kitchen, she laid out carefully for him the clothing he had worn when he first appeared. She tucked him in for the night.

"Helen, my lovely goddess," he murmured, half asleep. "I will miss you."

"Sleep well, my sweet. You have a difficult journey to-morrow."

❊

At dawn they struck out together on the fire road. At the top of the hill near the oak tree, they started down the overgrown path. They trampled through the brush arm-in-arm. She steadied her steps with the alpenstock clasped in her right hand.

Halfway down the hill, they were enveloped in whirling fog. She laid the alpenstock on the ground, removed the box from the pocket of her khakis, and gave it to him.

"Goodbye, Franz. I love you. I release you. Go in peace, and compose your exquisite music." She kissed him on his cheek.

"Goodbye, Helen, and God bless you. You have been a marvelous cousin to me." But his voice was already breaking off. He had turned away, and was peering into the distance. She clutched his arm. Then, in an instant, she realized there was only empty air in her hand. He was no longer there. Where was he?

She remained behind alone in that waste and welter of

which she was so terrified. The fog was so thick that she could see only inches in front of her. Was that a mountain lion crashing behind her in the brush? She grabbed the alpenstock and ran, panic-stricken, up the hill. Thistles stung her ankles. Why hadn't she thought to ask the rebbe for protection from wild animals? Would this adventure end in her own death scream?

The sun appeared, and she could see the top of the hill. She sprinted up the slope. At the summit along the edge of the fire road, she paused, panting. Her legs wobbled under her, and she collapsed on the ground. She wailed, a long and heartrending "Ahhhh, Franz, Franz," as disconsolate as a keener at an Irish wake. Her lament reverberated in the canyon, until it was sucked into the muffling fog below, and died out.

She laid the alpenstock on her lap, and fingered its handle carved with an intricate design of oak leaves. The next moment, she spotted an athletic man probably in his fifties, with a barbered gray beard, walking briskly on the fire road. He was dressed in black sweats and New Balance running shoes. Waving his hand, he hallooed.

"Good morning. Do you live in this neck of the woods? My name is Russ Massoth. I just bought that house over there"—he pointed toward the main road.

She stood up, balancing on the alpenstock.

"Why, yes, I do," she managed to reply, although the words were halting and inarticulate. She wondered if her face was wrinkled and puffy.

"That's an interesting walking stick. It reminds me of a curio handed down in my own family."

"It's an antique, from Vienna, I think."

"Well then, we have two things in common already. Could you introduce me to this incredible scenery? I'm sorry, I didn't catch your name."

"Helen Bramer. Yes, I can show you a beautiful trail."

She set off by his side, and their talk was slow and cautious, places they had been, seas they wished to sail.

Perhaps Reb Mendel had included extra Hebrew letters in his blessing, just for her.

"Thank you, rebbe," she whispered under her breath.

GaGa's Piano

I

THREE IN THE MORNING, in mid-June. Patricia startled awake. Two-and-half-year-old Kayla, the daughter of Patricia's niece, Jessica, was screaming, "GaGa, GaGa!" Patricia had put the child down for the night in the crib installed by her husband Scott in a corner of the guest bedroom adjacent to their own. This room was already furnished with a twin bed, and there had been long discussions of whether the child was ready to sleep in it. So far she had not climbed out of the crib. Patricia stumbled out of bed, hurried into the guest room, and switched on the light.

"GaGa, scary bear get Kay-ya." The child was standing up, gripping the bars of the crib. "Where's the bear, honey?" Sobbing, Kayla pointed to the bed. Patricia tiptoed over and grunted as she pretended to pick up a heavy object.

"OK, sweetheart, I've caught him, I'll take him outside, where he can sleep with his bear family." She stepped into the hallway and walked to the front door, making a great noise of opening and closing it. She doubled back to Kayla's room. The child was now sitting up, her back wedged against the bars of the crib. She sucked her thumb and whimpered.

"All gone," Patricia cooed, as she petted the child's

head, laid her gently on her back, and covered her with a pink polka-dot plush blanket. Kayla sank immediately into the serene slumber of toddlerhood.

Patricia returned to the four-poster marital bed. Scott lay awake under the star-pattern Amish quilt. He cuddled next to her, and after a few moments, murmured,

"Patti darling, I know we've talked about this before, but honestly you seem to love this kid more than anyone else, maybe even more than you love me. You know she's not your responsibility. You're not her mother or her grand-mother."

Patricia blinked back tears. "I think it's that I always wanted children, and it never happened. And she just seems to love me the most. I feel so close to this child, whose sweet mother wanted me to see her baby born."

Scott fondled her hair and kissed her on the lips. "I love you more than my life. But I'm telling you to be careful not to cross an emotional line. It's not your job to raise her. She may as well live here, the amount of time we baby-sit."

She trusted his judgment, and sensed his concern, or was it a tinge of anger? She wanted to please him, to be a good wife—it had been so long before God had blessed her with a good husband, through the intercession, she was convinced, of her favorite saint, Anthony of Padua, the patron saint of lost things. Of course Scott must come first in her affections, in her life. She wondered if he was right, if she was too involved in Kayla's upbringing.

II

As the mythical Mother Goose clucked over her brood, so the fifty-five-year-old childless Patricia fussed over her piano students. On three days a week during the school year, after finishing her day-job in a county government office, she gave half-hour piano lessons to children from four to seven o'clock in the spacious prairie-style home she shared with Scott in a new development in Spencerville, Illinois. The last census had reported a population of one hundred thousand, the largest township in downstate farm country.

A typical scene would unfold. A seventh-grade girl trudged along the sidewalk on an April afternoon, reaching Patricia's driveway ten minutes before the five o'clock lesson time. The girl would open the unlocked side door, tiptoe inside, and sit on the floral damask sofa in the living room. In the music room, a boy, age nine, hunched over the keys of the 1922 Steinway grand. Patricia's encouraging words floated over the halting notes, many of them botched, of a Clementi sonatina. "Better than last week but you need to practice more."

The girl might leaf through her assigned score, a movement from a Mozart sonata, or stare out the window at the piebald cat stalking a sparrow near the bird feeder. She would repeat to herself the excuses for why she had not practiced enough that week. Her mother constantly pointed out that the charming Taiwanese girl who lived down the block had more discipline, and why couldn't her daughter do as well? And then it was the girl's turn to enter the sanctum of the music room. Thank goodness this section was adagio because her fingers were not nearly agile enough for the passages marked allegro. When the half hour was over, she stared at the ivory keys of the piano, too flustered to look at her teacher.

Patricia smiled. She removed her bifocals, letting them dangle from a red neck cord.

"For next week, sight read the third movement very slowly. Set the metronome at sixty. And promise you'll practice at least a half hour every day."

The girl, studying the planks of the oak floor, mumbled, "Yes, ma'am."

"Good, and don't forget, the final recital is only six weeks away. You are progressing splendidly. You'll be a star performer."

Patricia had the magic touch with all her pupils, especially the shy ones. Year after year, her students won honors at Festival, the annual Illinois state piano competition. In some way she articulated only vaguely, imparting European classical music to new generations had become an all-absorbing vocation.

The oxymoronic phrase "pop culture" irritated her. This deluge of inane images and sounds resembled a toxic sludge surging toward a pristine sanctuary, smashing through doors and windows and burying the interior in mud and offal. She constructed a sturdy barricade to keep undisturbed her tidy corner of the tradition, and she looked forward to her scheduled retirement in five years, a modest pension, and the leisure to expand her roster of students.

III

Both sides of Patricia's family, the Hills and the Browns, had settled in Spencerville generations ago. There were no frills in her childhood home. Her mother was a devout daily-rosary Catholic who shepherded her two daughters to Saturday confession and Sunday Mass, and placed them in the parish grade school. Little Patti had obvious musical ability, and there had been piano lessons with a woman who had a music degree from Sacred Heart, the local Catholic liberal arts college. At the request of this woman, the college allowed the girl access to a practice room, as the family could not afford to buy even a bargain-priced used spinet. At twelve, she already could play from memory and with strong technique the Beethoven *Appassionata* and *Pathetique* sonatas. Two years later, the lessons were abruptly dropped. Her father was floundering in his job selling plumbing supplies over a tri-state territory, and money was tight. Patricia graduated from her parish grade school, but then her parents enrolled her in the tuition-free public high school, a middling place catering to average students. Her sister Linda, four years younger, was yanked out of the Catholic school after the fourth grade, and the next eight years she attended public school.

For those four high school years Patricia wandered in a wasteland, dreaming about music, humming the polyphonic melodies, fluttering her fingers in the air pretending to play. The college practice room was still available, but without a teacher her former strict daily regimen atrophied to an occasional half-hour of haphazard sight-reading. At the end of her senior year, as if through a miracle of St. Anthony, she found her lost music. On the strong recommendation of that early piano teacher, Sacred Heart gave her a full scholarship to study piano, though she had bungled the audition.

IV

Mother Beata, a Benedictine nun, the head of the music department of ten instructors and forty students, took Patricia in hand. No tender mercies, but a rigorous gladiatorial boot camp. The teenager was thrown immediately into the arena, daily piano lessons, accompanist to the choral students, and public solo recital performances.

"You must practice, practice, practice, no excuses, my dear, your talent is a gift from God, use it for His glory." The martinet nun could have been a twelfth-century Hildegard exhorting a postulant.

At the Easter recital in the college concert hall, fili-greed with Baroque marble cupid heads and furnished with maroon velvet chairs, two minutes into the ten-minute Chopin Scherzo Number 2, Patricia flubbed an intricate arpeggio run. She panicked, stood up, and almost tripping over the Jansen bench, wobbled backstage. A frowning Mother Beata barred her way.

"I can't remember it," said Patricia, gasps convulsing her chest.

No coddling from the fierce nun, who barked at her, "You must remember it. Now pull yourself together, go back out there, and play it."

As if in a trance, Patricia glided back to the Steinway grand, sat down, began over again, and played the piece all the way through.

As a seemingly dead plant, its leaves brittle and brown from drought, can spring forth green and lush when finally the gentle rains come, so Patricia flourished. There was another reason, too, for throwing herself into practice. Things at home were awry. Linda, only sixteen, was pregnant and had disappeared for four months to give birth at a Catholic unwed mothers' home in the countryside. The baby boy had been spirited into the labyrinth of sealed secret adoptions, no questions asked, no information given. Patricia's mother was more obsessed than ever with Catholicism, and her father simply stayed away, supposedly working his sales routes, though his commissions were minuscule.

After three years, Mother Beata's frown brightened into the beatific smile implied by her name. She sent her protégée to Chicago to audition for entrance into the American Conservatory of Music. Patricia was awarded a full scholarship, and her instructor was to be Miss Florence Abbott, a Juilliard graduate who had studied with a world-famous Russian-Jewish émigré. Patricia's stipend included full room and board at the Three Arts Club, an all-female rooming house catering to young women studying the arts, an easy ten-minute ride on the "L" to the Conservatory.

And now Patricia's professional training began. Piano lessons took place in a bare room furnished with a Steinway vertical under a fluorescent-lit ten-foot ceiling, on the far side a milk-glass tilt turn window looking out on an alleyway, a steam radiator clanking out heat on the wall near the door. The muffled sounds of students drilling scales in a maze of identical practice rooms permeated the air. To her the place seemed a humanist villa in Fiesole, the walls frescoed with scenes of the Muses, the windows revealing a landscape of cypress trees and olive groves.

Patricia would sit rigidly on the piano bench, with Miss Abbott sitting just behind. Sometimes the older woman would stand up and splay her own lined and blue-veined virtuoso hands over the young woman's smooth pink apprentice hands. Then she would step to the side. Meeting Patricia's eyes and touching her gray hair braided into a bun, and then her heart, her arms and her fingertips, she coaxed her protégée in a soft hypnotic voice, as from some virginal ethereal realm.

"My sweet, pay close attention, music comes from God, to our intellect, thence to our heart, to our arms, to our hands, out to our fingertips, to the keys of this sublime instrument."

Then she raised her thin arms, palms outward, in a priestly blessing. "You must engage your mind fully, you must concentrate, you must practice daily many, many hours. Learn one Bach fugue, analyze it thoroughly, note by note, each note exactly as the great man composed it, as God dictated the notes to him."

The pupil sat with rapt attention, absorbing every precious word from this God-sent mentor. Miss Abbott continued her homily.

"The master crafted each piece with meticulous workmanship, in perfect Pythagorean ratios, the music of the spheres. If you unriddle a single Bach fugue, you will internalize its structure. You will learn easily all the rest of Bach, and all the rest of Music. Commit every detail to memory and then play spontaneously."

Patricia was determined to please this woman, who was somehow more than mortal, who seemed a fairy godmother with a white-magic wand of protection and guidance. She wished this idyll never to end: thrice-weekly morning lessons with Miss Abbott, choral conducting class on the other two weekday mornings, every afternoon the cocoon of focused practice, on Sunday afternoons a private piano recital to perform or a ten-voice chorus to conduct.

The occasional brief trips home to Spencerville alarmed her. At dinner, her mother obsessively catalogued her objections to the Vatican II changes, and complained about the naughty grade school children to whom she attempted to teach catechism on Saturday mornings. Her father was silent, his mouth set in numb fury. Linda's permanent expression was a noncommittal smirk. Her necklines were low, revealing D-cup cleavage, and her miniskirts exposed her thighs all the way up to her panties. Everyone was relieved because she had landed a secure secretarial job with the county, but there were inklings that she was barhopping and hanging out with a wild crowd.

Patricia graduated with a bachelor's degree, a piano major and choral conducting minor. Her family did not attend the ceremony as the trip was too expensive, what with the high price of gas and the prohibitive cost of a Chicago hotel. The dean's office found her a one-room walkup in a greystone in Lincoln Park.

V

Now Patricia cobbled together a frugal bohemian life for seven years, teaching music in a Catholic girls' elementary school and finding ad-hoc venues in which to perform for pittance fees, a small-town girl struggling to make good in the metropolis.

At a chamber music recital at the Chicago Cultural Center, the program Mozart and Brahms piano quartets, a man twenty years older introduced himself and asked her out. He was a junior partner in a family investment firm, already an income beneficiary of a grandfather's trust. His was a world of chef-prepared and servant-ministered formal sit-down dinners in Gold Coast high-rises, opening nights at the Lyric Opera, and charity galas at the Art Institute. In spite of his family's opposition, he proposed marriage, promising to finance Patricia's musical career. She accepted, though the ceremony would not be officiated by a priest. It was all so much a fairy tale, and she the Cinderella. Two weeks after her beau placed a five-carat diamond on the ring finger of her left hand, an anonymous unstamped letter slid under her front door revealed his ongoing dalliances with two other women. She returned the ring and backed out of the wedding. In the confessional an elderly Irish priest told her in an oracular brogue that God had rescued her, that this unblessed union would have consigned her to Hell, certainly in this life, and very possibly in the next. Though she realized the priest was right, still she wept into her pillow every night.

Four months later Patricia's father was incapacitated by a stroke. In Spencerville it was expected that unmarried daughters would live with and nurse their parents in old age. Linda had married and established a home with her husband Reese. So Patricia moved back to Spencerville and settled into her old attic bedroom.

How disappointing, the cosmopolitan rainbow of her city life fading back into the colorless air of the flat, drab prairie. Through family contacts, she landed a county government clerical job. The tasks were boring, and her co-workers small-minded and backstabbing, but the hours were regular. Once she left the office, there was freedom to swim in the waters of the regional music scene, church choirs and musicals and Viennese light opera, where all acclaimed her a genius. One monotonous year followed another. No possibility of marriage in such a provincial town.

She helped her mother caretake her father for five years until his death. A decade later, her mother was diagnosed with pancreatic cancer. Patricia took a leave from work and stayed with her mother around the clock. Linda came over with flowers a few times, but fled after a half-hour, bawling, "I can't stand to see mom like this!" In six months the swift-metastasizing tumors had done their deadly work. Immediately after the funeral the bungalow was sold, and the $50,000 in proceeds split between the two sisters. Linda went on an exuberant spending spree, and was back to ground zero within the year. Patricia opened a five-year CD for $20,000, and the rest she spent on new clothes and furniture for an apartment.

Soon after Patricia's mother died, Scott Polk had joined the church choir she directed. He was a widower, a trial attorney, with one son from his first marriage, now away at college. Scott's untrained baritone voice developed artful control under her expert tutelage. He came, he sang, and she conquered his heart. They envisioned a life together of elegant sufficiency, enriched by books and music. The couple had married in a solemn high nuptial Catholic Mass six years ago.

VI

Linda lived five miles away, near the old railroad yard, in a double-wide with three rescue cats. She had thirty years in with the county, and planned to retire in ten years with a pension greater than her salary. Her daughter Jessica had been born late by Spencerville standards, when Linda was thirty. Reese had skipped out when Jessica was two. Linda had in hand a divorce decree and numerous demands for child support, but the money never seemed to materialize, nor was Reese interested in visiting his only child.

Aunt Patti doted on Jessica, spending time with her, buying her dolls and clothes, driving her to Chicago to visit the museums and to revel in the palatial ambience of the Walnut Room at Marshall Field's. During her teens, the girl started to party with a slacker clique of cocaine-snorting, acting-out peers. Three years ago, a few weeks before high school graduation, Jessica became pregnant after a one-night stand with a muscular tattooed young man of twenty-five, who worked the graveyard shift as a private security guard at an industrial park.

Patricia had learned the disturbing news one Sunday afternoon from Linda, as the two sisters cleaned up the kitchen after a student recital held at Patricia's home. Linda could be relied upon to help with post-recital hospitality, to concoct lime sherbet-and-7Up punch and to arrange store-bought cookies on lacy paper doilies on Patricia's wedding-gift china platters.

Patricia felt faint. Was getting "knocked up" a family curse that would repeat generation to generation? Patricia let out a drawn-out "Oh no," and a reproach slipped out unthinkingly.

"After all my efforts to instill in her good morals, and love for the higher things, this is how she repays me! I mean us, of course. What's wrong with our family? Can't we ever do anything in the proper order, in the right way?"

Linda said, "Get real, Patti. There's nothing wrong with our family. Sex is natural, and I'm not ashamed."

Patricia said, "I suppose she'll give the baby up for adoption."

Linda clanked coffee cups as she loaded them in the dishwasher. "I'll take her to Planned Parenthood for an abortion, then she can get on with her life."

Patricia blanched. "What? You told her to get an abortion?"

Linda usually glossed over conflict with an agreeable smile and then did what she wanted anyway. But her mouth was now set in a grim frown. "Don't get all mushy Catholic on me. You know the church is hopelessly out of date on this. Don't you dare say anything to her against the idea. It's not your place."

But the headstrong Jessica had a plan of her own: to go it alone as a single mother. She requested that both her mother Linda and her Aunt Patti be present in the hospital delivery room. Patricia heard the newborn girl's first cries, and cradled the infant in her arms.

And now, as a toddler, Kayla most often demanded neither her MaMa, her mother Jessica, nor her NaNa, her grandmother Linda, but her GaGa—only her great-aunt Patricia would do. "Where GaGa?" Wails and flailing of fists and feet, till GaGa materialized.

Patricia would bounce Kayla on her knee and sing to her, a favorite song from Barney, the purple dinosaur, about the raindrops transformed into lemon drops and gum-drops. Squealing and clapping her hands, the little girl opened her mouth wide and thrust her face toward an imaginary sky.

"More," she insisted.

She reveled in the magic of GaGa's music room.

"Kayla, would you like to play the piano?" Patricia would place her on the bench. The child stood on her sturdy legs, banging on the ivory keys. She loved Patricia's recordings of Brahms symphonies and Puccini operas. What benign spirit had kindled such a fancy in this youngster? No one knew. MaMa Jessica and NaNa Linda blasted the bass speakers on their stereos, Jessica lip-syncing Eminem, Linda slow-dancing to the Eagles and Barry Manilow.

VII

Mother Beata, at age ninety-six, lived in the Benedictine motherhouse in the countryside, fifty miles outside town in a small second story room overlooking a flower garden. She was wheelchair-bound now, cared for tenderly by the younger nuns. The room was furnished with a spinet piano and an antique pine dry sink in which many musical scores were stashed. Every day the wrinkled nun would sit in her wheelchair, warmed by blankets, gazing at the piano keys. Sometimes a caretaker would take out some of the scores and show them to the elderly woman, who nodded feebly and whispered the names of composers, Chopin or Beethoven or Bach.

Patricia visited Mother Beata twice yearly, just before Easter and during the Christmas season. "What would you like to hear, Mother?" Patricia would ask, and the nun would smile and nod, and whisper "Anything, darling." So Patricia would dig into the pile of scores, find melancholic

Chopin or percussive Beethoven or mathematical Bach, which she had once memorized and performed but no longer knew by heart, and sight-read the pieces. The nuns and the caretakers and the clerical staff would come running and crowd the room, eager to hear the impromptu recital. Visitors would start to congregate outside in the hall. For the finale, Patricia would play the instrumental part of the Franck "Panis Angelicus" at Easter, and at Christmas, the Adolphe Adam "O Holy Night," and Patricia's college girlfriend, Sister Mary Francis, with her trained soprano voice, would lead off the solo. All the crowd would join in the chorus, the voices heard by the gardeners and the visitors on the grounds outside, who would stop still and gaze upward toward Mother Beata's window. Was this a Millet painting?

And so, over Palm Sunday weekend, Patricia prepared for her visit to the motherhouse. It was Saturday, and Scott was at the office working against deadline on a legal brief. The phone rang, Jessica on the line, blubbering.

"I can't find Mom. Please, please take Kayla. This is last minute, and I'll make it up to you. But the hospital called me, my friend Britney's just been admitted, you met her, remember? She's overdosed on something, I need to get over there."

Patricia sighed. Kayla was too young to visit the motherhouse, and yet the appointment was set-in-stone, impossible to reschedule, so she'd have to take the child with her. Jessica took seriously the responsibility of raising her daughter on meager wages as a receptionist in a dental office, and Patricia sympathized with the exhausted young woman. She and Scott kicked in half Jessica's rent on a rundown cottage in a neighborhood of ninety-year-old shotgun houses, all peeling paint and sagging porches. Though this shabbiness might alarm a middle-class rubbernecker unfamiliar with the locale, in fact the crime rate was low. But Patricia worried that Jessica was still involved with low-lives. This frantic telephone call seemed proof that Jessica hadn't severed ties with her old druggie circle.

Within fifteen minutes Jessica's junker Chevy Malibu was parked in Patricia's driveway, and the young mother lifted Kayla from the car and set her down on the concrete. Kayla spotted Patricia standing in the doorway. The child screeched "GaGa!" and ran over and grasped Patricia's legs. The great-aunt caressed the little girl's hair.

Jessica bussed Patricia on the cheek, said a hurried "Thanks, I'll make it up to you, Aunt Patti," and turned to go.

"Wait, Jessica, tell me what's going on."

"I told you, I have to go to the hospital to help a friend."

The words came out of Patricia's mouth before she could censure them. "I hope you're not still hanging out with that bad crowd. You've a child to think about."

Jessica's protest was immediate and loud. "I don't need you to scold me! You know I'm a good mother. I thought you were on my side."

Patricia managed a stiff smile. "I'm sorry, Jessica. I shouldn't have said that, I take it back. You're an excellent mother. It's good of you to be there for a friend."

Jessica nodded acknowledgment, and waved her right hand, gabbling, "Bye, bye," to her daughter, as she sprinted back to the car, then floored the accelerator, peeling away from the curb.

Patricia dressed Kayla, and tossed plush animal toys and alphabet blocks into a canvas tote bag to keep the child amused. During the hour drive the little girl fell asleep, and when Patricia woke her she fussed at first, but then calmed down and walked willingly hand in hand from the parking lot into the lobby of the motherhouse. The teenage girl on duty at the front desk welcomed them, and exclaimed over the pretty toddler dressed in a pink cotton frilly dress, black patent Mary Janes, and grasping a worn, pink fluffy bunny. There was a special room and a babysitter for children, would Patricia like the adorable princess to join the other kids? Patricia said yes, in a little while, but first she'd like Mother Beata to meet Kayla.

Patricia walked into Mother Beata's room with Kayla. She let go of the child's hand to approach Mother Beata sitting in her wheelchair, and bent down to hug and kiss the old nun.

Kayla stared from the doorway and sucked her thumb. Then she mewled, "GaGa," and then shrieked several times, "GaGa, GaGa!"

Patricia took Kayla's hand and approached the wheelchair. "Kayla, sweetheart, say hello to Mother Beata. She was GaGa to me when I was growing up."

Kayla quieted, and sucking her thumb, looked dubiously at the old woman, who in her turn examined the tiny visitor, puzzlement, or was it dismay? on her dried-apple-doll face.

Patricia picked up the thread of her usual conversation with Mother Beata.

"What would you like to hear, Mother? How about Chopin today?"

She let go of Kayla's hand, walked over to the dry sink, removed a well-thumbed Schirmer collection of Chopin Etudes, and settled at the piano. Kayla toddled toward the piano bench.

"Kay-ya pay, GaGa."

"No honey, not now. You can watch GaGa play."

"No, no." Kayla pulled on the legs of the piano bench.

All this time Mother Beata sat complacently in her wheelchair. She didn't seem to understand who this child was, but she didn't seem particularly to mind the disturbance.

Patricia signaled to a young nun she knew from her prior visits, who stood just inside the room.

"Could you please take Kayla to the children's room? Kayla, this nice lady will take you to play with the other children."

The young nun smiled and walked over and took Kayla's hand. "C'mon you precious, I have some nice candy for you. And we have lots of toys and games here."

Instinctually, Kayla trusted this gentle blue-eyed young woman. Clenching her bunny a little tighter, the child left without further protest.

Patricia played for an hour, as the crowd gathered, and finally all joined in the Franck chorus. When the recital was over, the crowd dispersed, and Patricia was left alone with Mother Beata. She set the piano bench close to the wheelchair, sat down, and took into her own hands the nun's arthritis-gnarled hands.

"Mother, that child is my niece Jessica's daughter, you remember Jessica, she's all grown up now. I told you my worries, she's raising the little girl all by herself, she has no money. I see so much of myself in the child. She has musical talent, and needs careful nurturing. But my dear husband Scott, I'm afraid he may not like me to get enmeshed in my family troubles."

The old nun's eyes were vacant, gazing into some far distance. Then she whispered, haltingly, so that Patricia strained to understand the words.

"I know you, don't I? I taught you, you had talent. Long years ago now."

"Yes mother, you were my salvation. Saint Anthony sent you to me."

The old nun smiled, and closed her eyes. Her head drooped a bit, and then she was asleep.

VIII

Six weeks later, on a Sunday afternoon in June, Scott, a history buff, sat reading the McCullough biography of John Adams in the leather club chair in the living room. Patricia reclined on the sofa, and studied the score of a Beethoven piano trio, while tapping out the meter with her fingertips. They were watching Kayla while Jessica shopped at the mall with Linda.

Kayla ran around in circles, bobbing and hopping, somersaulting and giggling. Suddenly, she flung her right arm straight out and pointed with her tiny index finger to the built-in bookcase crammed with Scott's books.

"Kay-ya read, GaGa." She pulled out several hardcover Harvard Classics from the bottom shelf and piled them on the floor. She grasped Plutarch's *Lives* and opening it upside down, sat there, gazing solemnly up at the two adults and then looking down at the book. "Read, read, Kay-ya read."

"Yes honey, soon you'll be reading." Patricia imagined this precocious child in forty-odd years, a classics scholar, a tenured professor at the University of Chicago, all because of GaGa and Uncle Scott.

Kayla clamored her joy, and dragging the book, bounced up and ran over to Scott. She knocked over Patricia's glass of diet Pepsi on the coffee table. Ice cubes and brown liquid spattered everywhere, on the book, the table, the oak-planked floor, the club chair, Kayla's unicorn-pattern T-shirt. Patricia scurried to the kitchen for paper towels. Scott didn't scold Kayla, but pressed the pages of the book and left it open on top of an antique cupboard to dry out, only shaking his head a little. She guessed his frustration. He had paid top dollar for the leather-bound, gilt-edged set of classics.

Early on the following Saturday, Jessica dropped off Kayla at GaGa's house for the entire weekend. She and Linda were attending the wedding of a distant Brown cousin whose family ran a prosperous hog farm a hundred miles away. They planned to overnight and return late on Sunday. In mid-morning, Patricia drove the child for the first time to the public library, a sprawling four-story concrete government building that had replaced the stone, neoclassical Carnegie-era edifice she remembered from her girlhood.

The children's room had been designed to accommodate cherubs and hobbits: pint-sized plastic chairs and tables in bold reds and blues and greens. Patricia selected two Beatrix Potter tales. She wanted to expose Kayla to glossy illustrated Edwardian British children's books that were shelved in the private libraries of Chicago mansions. Patricia had given piano recitals, Chopin and Schubert and Debussy, during afternoon teas in these great Romanesque Revival brick and stone houses, her patronesses in little silk dresses and kitten-heel pumps, their Catherine Deneuve hair swept into chignons belle époque.

"Look, Kayla, aren't these rabbits adorable? And see, here's a picture of mean Mr. McGregor's boot." Kayla's taste ran to Saturday morning cartoon characters. She was sucking her thumb and stamping her foot.

"No, no. Scooby Doo!"

"No darling, Beatrix Potter. Peter Rabbit. Yummy blackberries and cute round cabbages."

"NO! NO!"

"Flopsy, Mopsy, Cottontail and—"

"NOOO!"

She whined until Patricia found the popular TV Great Dane. After twenty minutes, Kayla had chosen six books. Patricia added *Peter Rabbit* to the stack. All the books would be kept at GaGa's house, to be read to Kayla whenever the little girl stayed over.

Kayla clutched Patricia's hand as they walked back to the entrance. Patricia piled the books on the checkout counter. The child begged to be picked up to watch, and Patricia obliged. When the librarian, a pink-faced, overweight woman reeking of Zest soap, reached for the books to scan their barcodes, Kayla howled, "Mine," and wriggling to escape Patricia's arms, kicked one of the books to the floor. The librarian grimaced and ducked below the counter to retrieve the book.

"What a darling little girl," she said as she processed the books, never once looking up.

Patricia glanced uneasily at the line of patrons waiting for their turns. Some smiled, but others scowled, seeming to disapprove. Patricia flinched. There was always that nagging residuum of poisonous shame, that she and her family were somehow not-normal, not-good-enough, that they didn't know how to bring up children who behaved properly and who achieved great things.

On the way home, Patricia stopped at the fourth-generation German bakery downtown and bought an oversized piece of Scott's favorite, the bakery's secret-recipe apple strudel.

IX

And now, in the dark, Patricia snuggled against Scott, searching for words to respond to him. Yes, she thought, he's upset, and he's justified. After all, he had already raised a child, and had married her on the implicit understanding there would be no more children. He had brought this up before, and she thought that his words were becoming more forceful. Patricia knew she must somehow frame an answer.

Surely God would forgive her if she fudged the question. She assured herself that this situation was only temporary, that it would stop as soon as Jessica got on her feet and Kayla started school. But that was a fib that both she and Scott knew was untrue. They both realized this entanglement would last as long as life.

Must she make a choice between Scott and Kayla? Perhaps it was time to pull back, to have a conversation with Jessica about "boundaries." But no, no, the newspeak of therapists was completely wrong. The situation was ideal, as if through divine grace she had found a precious lost thing. And how could she explain the heart of the matter to herself, and to him? This prattling blonde cherub, blood of her blood, filled up a gaping chasm deep in her gut, where a desert wind whistled through, and a stern voice lectured her:

> *Alas, it is late, too late for you, Patricia.*
> *You are old, your womb is barren. There is no hope.*
> *The ancient times of prophecy and miracles are no more.*

To which a still small voice whispered:

> *God has endowed little Kayla with prodigious musical talent.*
> *You, Patricia, must bequeath your sacred knowledge to her.*
> *The ancient times of prophecy and miracles*
> *live on in GaGa's transcendent piano.*

She nestled closer to Scott and opened her mouth to speak, but he had drifted back to sleep, snoring gently. Tomorrow, with Saint Anthony's help, she would find the right words.

CURIOUS AFFAIRS

The Seraphita Sonata

Margaret cradled the receiver of the retro black dial telephone. What a delight to hear Albert's hello.

"I'm thrilled to be here. I can't wait to see you again," she said.

"Come over to the Seraphita at four o'clock. You can watch me practice the sonata with James. It rains every afternoon, so make sure you take an umbrella."

"And what if you're not there yet? Where should I wait?"

"Simply go on in. The doors are never locked. Mildred, poor old thing, trusts the universe."

A few hours earlier Margaret had checked into this room at the Black Spruce Inn in Lake Placid, New York. The bed-and-breakfast proved to be a rambling, white-clapboard Victorian house, stuffed with period furniture and paintings. A glassed-in porch chock-a-block with chaise longues was wrapped around its front facade. In an average town the inn would be easy to find. But the mansions here did not advertise much: no mailbox names or numbers, the houses set back on expansive lawns, far from the prying eyes of curious passersby. She found the inn only after circling and backtracking twice.

The flight from Los Angeles had been torment. The departure time was weather-delayed by four hours, and the plane experienced gut-wrenching turbulence, thumping and diving and shaking from violent thunderstorms.

Margaret missed her connecting flight in Newark and overnighted in the terminal, sprawled over two plastic-upholstered chairs at a remote gate where the puddle-jumpers parked, with a motley of stranded passengers. Her sleep had been fitful and her body wracked with joint pain. The short flight to Albany this morning had at least been uneventful. She gobbled down a lavish country breakfast at Grandma's restaurant near the airport, and as a special treat to throw off the misery of the last twenty-four hours, indulged in homemade apple pie and vanilla ice cream. To her delight the three hour drive in a flimsy subcompact rental car unfolded a landscape of ever more primordial mountains until it seemed she was at the edge of some mythic castellated kingdom.

The proprietor, a gray-bearded man in his fifties with that harassed look of all B&B owners, had greeted her perfunctorily, and supplied her with a skeleton key for an upstairs bedroom. Apparently the teenage bellhop had called in sick, and so, frowning and panting, the owner lugged her suitcase up the twenty stairs. A thirty-minute soak in the claw-foot tub filled with steaming water and rose-scented bath gel, and a two-hour nap in the four-poster bed revived her. Into her sleep stole a gentle healing dream, the details of which eluded her on waking. She sank into the velvet upholstery of a rosewood armchair and thumbed through a glossy tourist guide. There were photos of the lake, and of wildlife, and rhapsodic descriptions of restaurants. One whole page was devoted to a description and photographs of the giant Cecropia moth, indigenous to this area, and quite a favorite with visitors. And then Albert had telephoned.

Margaret had hesitated before accepting Albert's invitation. The trip was expensive. She was using half her personal days off and almost her entire vacation budget. The annual summer arts festival was in progress, and Albert was scheduled to give a recital at the Seraphita Arts Center with his old graduate school friend, James Dolen. Both men were now tenured British literature professors: Albert a Chaucerian, James a specialist in the Lake Poets. Their hobby was chamber music performance: Albert a pianist, James a flutist. Their recital was not part of the regular schedule, those pricey concerts given by famous names. Rather, theirs was a private event underwritten by elite donors. Admission was free, but invitees were expected to contribute generously to the festival. Albert and James had been reimbursed for all travel expenses, and were each lodged in a separate summer lake cottage loaned by wealthy patrons.

Margaret Stine had known Albert Zimmer for over seven years. They had met at a Christmas extravaganza at the Getty Villa in Malibu. At that time, he had tenure at USC. Soon they were inseparable: classical music concerts and the opera, meals together, long walks he called "constitutionals." Often he organized impromptu Sunday afternoon chamber music gatherings at his home in Griffith Park, Mozart and Schubert and Brahms, trios and quartets and quintets, he playing his pre-WWI concert grand Steinway, his friends bringing their bowed string and woodwind instruments. She sat by his side at the piano and turned pages for him, and after the music she served petit fours and jasmine tea and lemonade to the guests.

She had never met a man who so charmed her, whose mind so harmonized with her own. His move to Teversham village near Cambridge, England three years ago had put six thousand miles between them. Two years previous to that transfer, USC had granted him a sabbatical to lecture as a visiting scholar at Trinity College in Cambridge. The post had resulted in an offer for a full professorship. Elated, Albert accepted. He had given one year notice to

USC, sold his LA home and his Steinway, and donated his personal library of three thousand volumes to a small liberal arts college in northern California. Now he was free to start over, to build an entire new life in ideal surroundings.

After his move, they telephoned and exchanged e-mails and even the occasional old-fashioned letter. She saved printed versions of his e-mails together with his letters in an album tucked away in a drawer scented with lavender. Last summer during a two-week visit to LA, he had stayed with a well-to-do male cousin in Encino and had spent the whole of both weekends with her.

He had found the B&B for her, only a few short blocks from the arts center. He had noted that "Seraphita" was a reference to an obscure Balzac supernatural novel, not much read today in respectable university circles. The center functioned also as a spiritual forum modeled after the Transcendentalists. She wondered if séances might be held there. He thought possibly so, as the owner, Mrs. Mildred Wright—in her nineties, the widow of a distinguished Yale medievalist—was, in his opinion, extraordinarily daft.

❈

Somewhere, bells struck the sixteen notes of the Big Ben melody, and then three chimes. If she left now, there would be plenty of time to explore a little, to find the Seraphita. She examined herself in the full-length cherrywood oval cheval mirror. Her oversized floral print tunic was meant to hide the ten pounds she had gained since Albert's LA visit a year ago. But did the deception work? Wouldn't he notice? Forty-five was the new thirty, everyone said. Still, it was possible she had toppled over the divide, from desirable coquette into middle-aged frump.

She set out on the road that fronted the inn. Forty-foot pines lined the road. The conifer needles stirring in the strong breeze resembled the sound of a waterfall. The sun played hide and seek with fluffy cumulus clouds, now piling and darkening in the middle distance to form a thunderhead.

In less than a half mile, on the left side, a substantial property of several acres was visible. The expanse of un-kempt lawn was bounded by a rusted wrought iron fence choked by masses of brambly bushes. Beyond grew a thick grove of blue-green spruce trees, a tangle of new silvery growth and dead brown branches. Patches of white clap-board behind and above these trees gave the impression of a sizable house.

A dollop of poppy-red caught her eye. A male Cecropia moth, his wings spanning six inches, rested on the top rung of the fence, near a rickety gate. How exciting to spot one on her first stroll outside. The moth's feathery red anten-nae oscillated at some lepidopteran microcosmic frequency. Odd that this nocturnal being would linger out here in the daylight. Next to him, a weathered gray sign dangled from the fence. Stenciled in pallid orange were an arrow and the letters S R P IT. This must be the place.

She undid the rusty latch, and the gate groaned for-ward. Thunder rolled miles away. A few warm raindrops splattered her hair and dripped down her face. She plunged into the gloom under the canopy of the spruce trees. Some-one had once laid out stepping stones that were now over-grown with long slippery grasses. The path skirted a pond engulfed by water lilies, the arched cups of their waxy white flowers floating on thick green scum.

Just beyond was the porch of the house. She clacked a bronze knocker, the head of a laughing Renaissance humanist, perhaps Boccaccio. No answer. She turned the knob, and the monumental wood door opened silently, as if well-oiled and often used.

"Halloo. Anybody home?"

No answer, no sign of life.

After wiping her feet on a bristly horsehair mat, she crossed the threshold into an entry hall. Spongy pine planks sank beneath her feet. To the right was an enormous whitewashed room. A modern architect had knocked out walls and floors and opened some thirty-five feet of vertical space straight up to a glass skylight. Two ambulatories, their walls lined with books, circled the upper stories at the levels where floors had once been. The rain now pattered steadily on the skylight above and at the windows.

The room was filled with overstuffed sofas and leather armchairs. A concert grand piano with cabriole legs and a gleaming burled walnut case dominated a near corner. Nearby stood a mahogany cabinet, its top a slab of thick marble, dark green veined with amber. Intrigued, she walked over to examine it. What if someone should see her? They would think she was snooping. Well, let them. She was on vacation, far from the gossip of home. And, after all, Albert had given her permission.

She sat down on the Persian carpet and turned the gilt knob of the cabinet door. Inside was a stash of musical scores. She riffled through them. On the bottom lay an old book bound in scuffed brown leather. A threadbare blue silk ribbon peeked out. She pulled out the book, closed the cabinet, and plopped down on a sofa. A tug at the ribbon opened the book to a page filled with an old-fashioned cursive handwriting in a violet ink. A date was at the top. Could this be a diary?

> *16 June 1888   My darling Julia is coughing blood. Alas, she cannot last the summer. I play the piano for her in the evenings. This storm has broken my heart.*

The drumming of the rain on the skylight and against the windows intensified. Brilliant-white lightning bolts illuminated the gray murkiness of the room. Earsplitting thunder boomed. Southern California never experienced these bravura squalls; she found them harrowing. She set the diary on the floor, and reclined full length on the sofa for what seemed an eternity. Gradually the rain diminished, and the thunder subsided to a distant rumble. She stirred, stretched, and sat upright. No sounds but irregular raindrops in the still house—no clock ticking, no cat purring, no fire crackling. She picked up the diary.

> *18 June 1888   Dr. Trudeau has paid a call. There is no hope. I sense her despair. Last night, I played Liszt for her.*

Margaret fancied she heard a piano playing the Liszt *Liebestraum* in A Flat Major, a lament of unrequited passion. At thirteen she had drilled this piece under the strict tutelage of Mrs. Lazar, all the while dreaming of Gary, a boy in her algebra class. She loved Liszt. Where could the music be coming from? Not from the silent piano in this empty room. She studied her surroundings. At the far end of the room a solarium extended out. Three Adirondack chaise longues, their cedar frames overlaid with blue-striped cushions, were arranged there.

Alarmed, Margaret realized that a young woman, perhaps twenty years old, reclined on one of these chairs. A white cotton nightdress trimmed with lace fell gracefully over the length of her body. The girl gazed out the rain-spattered windows toward the spruce trees. Slowly she turned her head and looked straight at Margaret. Was it only Margaret's imagination that the girl's features seemed to resemble Margaret's own in Polaroids snapped a quarter century ago? Those photos were stuffed in albums and the color was streaking to yellow and sepia. Margaret had been teased often about her generic sweet-girl-next-door looks, and so too this girl might be classed. But unlike the Margaret of those pictures, she was waxy-pale and emaciated. Her blue eyes glittered with fever, and beads of perspiration glistened on her forehead.

Who was she? Had she been watching Margaret all this time? How embarrassing, to be caught out as the worst of all human types, a skulk, a sneak, prying into private cupboards and corners. But in some strange way, Margaret intuited that this listless girl did not notice or negatively judge the actions of other people. Even if she had been observing Margaret, there was no animosity in her enervated stare. Margaret decided there was no cause for anxiety.

The final pianissimo chords of the *Liebestraum* died out, and then, silence. Margaret got up to approach the girl, to introduce herself and to smooth over the situation. But the body was fading out gradually, the form that had appeared solid dissolving into wavy squiggles. Margaret watched, fascinated. After a minute, only a gossamer mist hovered over the chair.

Margaret was coming unglued, yet her curiosity propelled her toward the solarium to investigate. The air here felt at least twenty degrees cooler. The pungent smell of mold permeated the area. A hazy blue phosphorescent halo danced around the chair. Had a girl been lying in it? Had the sounds of a piano been real? Of course all these bizarre events must be mere hallucinations, caused by jet lag and exhaustion, and yet this place felt ensorcelled, and these happenings seemed somehow normal and commonplace.

"There you are." The familiar tenor voice startled her.

She spun around. Albert was grinning at her.

"I'm sorry," she said. "I couldn't help nosing around. I know I should have waited in the hall."

She walked over and kissed him on the top of his bald head. His height was a full three inches shorter than her five foot seven. Under his arm was a red leather portfolio, which he now deposited on an armchair. He hugged her around her ribs. A scent of rain and conifer clung to his damp turtleneck sweater.

"Mimi darling, you look marvelous." His manner was absentminded. He had adopted this pet name within a month of knowing her. They had attended *Bohème* together. Her little brother, when lisping his first baby words, had called her May-may.

"I've missed you," she said.

Albert did not answer. He removed sheet music from the portfolio. He propped open the lid of the piano, adjusted the music desk, and opened the fallboard, all in one seamless movement. Sitting on the bench, he positioned the sheet music.

"Tomorrow night we play the Reinecke *Undine Sonata*. Do you know it?"

"No, but you always surprise everyone with wonderful new things."

"German romanticism, all dark forest myths. A water sprite longs for a soul, and marries a mortal knight. But the fates will not allow the union, and it ends badly. Madness and suicide. The piano part has many fast runs—not so easy."

"This country reminds me of the Alps. As a girl, I read *Heidi* over and over. And the lake seems a natural place for water sprites."

"Yes, water, water everywhere."

He drew his diminutive chest up, took a deep breath,

and poised his pudgy hands a half foot above the ivory keys. And then he plunged full force into the arpeggios of the final movement, swirling over five octaves.

Margaret stretched out on the sofa, listening. Albert swayed on the bench, as if in a trance. The music ebbed and flowed and filled the room.

She glanced toward the solarium. Another dollop of poppy-red color. She rose and tiptoed over. A Cecropia moth rested on a window pane, flickering his wings as if in time with the sonata. That faint blue luminescence appeared over the chaise longue, gradually materializing into the figure of the young woman.

Margaret stepped wide of the figure, walked cautiously back to her sofa, and sat down. She wanted to tell Albert, but dared not disturb him. A moment later the moth fluttered into the room, and landed on the piano top. Albert halted in mid-chord. He jumped up, and pointed an accusing index finger at the moth.

"Mimi, why is this bat loose? Has it escaped from some belfry?"

"That's not a bat, it's a big moth, bigger than some bats."

"For the love of God, I cannot concentrate with creatures attacking me."

"He seems harmless enough. He's vibrating to your sonata."

Albert looked toward the solarium. The girl was plainly visible. Margaret braced herself for a third-degree interrogation of who she might be. But Albert did not seem to see the girl.

He scowled. "I cannot, indeed I will not, play in the company of Jurassic moths. Order it to depart at once."

"It's a male, and he adores your sonata. He might only leave if you stop playing."

Albert flounced into an armchair. Here comes one of

his lectures, Margaret thought, the habit of half a lifetime spent pontificating to college sophomores from a podium.

"Mimi, really, I thought you were on my side. How can I possibly play this sonata correctly? There is a time for everything under the sun, and for that matter, under the rain. Now is not the proper time for gargantuan plumose insects."

"I have no control over that moth, Albert. Besides, I'm not your wife or your colleague or even your page turner. Even if I knew what to do, it's not my job to take care of these things—or anything!—for you."

Albert glared at her.

Margaret felt that she had gone too far. Better to pacify him, she thought. She got up, and standing behind the back of his chair, put her arms lightly around his chest.

"Dear, dear Albert, I'm sorry. I'm so grateful to you for inviting me. I don't mean to argue with you. But I simply don't know what to do about the moth."

That apologetic tone, tacking into the wind of his ego, usually mollified him.

She returned to the sofa and sat down, facing him. Both of them looked toward the brilliant sunlight now streaming through the windows of the solarium. No moth, no girl, no mist. The light had chased away all nocturnal moths and phantoms. And, as if catching the phantom of an interrupted thought, Albert broke the silence.

"Move to Teversham and marry me."

This statement, so soon into their time together, disconcerted her. Typically this speech occurred as they said their goodbyes in telephone conversations, or as postscripts in his e-mails and letters, or last year, as she drove him to LAX. On their first date he had announced he was homosexual, but qualified that status as "seventy percent gay," by which he meant that he slept only with men but was attracted to, and sometimes fell in love, in an unattainable troubadour sense, with women of her English rose type, fair-skinned and blue-eyed.

"But you know it's impossible."

"Of course it is possible. The marriage would be patterned after an Enlightenment model. The logic is impeccable, the path well-trodden."

"I remember the first time you asked me to marry you. Five years ago, when I visited you in Cambridge, and we went sightseeing, and wandered around the ruined Roman villa. I vaguely knew the Romans conquered Britain, but that day it really hit home, the extent of their empire."

"And we got caught in a preternatural cloudburst, very like the cyclopean storms that rage here." Albert chimed in, his face softening into a smile.

"Of course no sex, you said. I said maybe, I'd think about it, after all, sex wasn't that important. And I've thought and thought, and of course sex is important."

"As I say, you could have your own lovers, and I will of course have my own lovers. Neither need know. An elegant solution."

"I don't want a marriage where I take other lovers. And if you had other lovers I would be so hurt."

"Mimi, you understand that my real love would always be you! Only you. The others, this one and that one, what are they but primitive biology, the lesser common Eros? Not so important, certainly not true love, not the greater philosophical Eros."

"The answer has to be no."

"The offer is always open, darling. If only you were a British countess, you would understand, you would say yes. We would have Tuesday at-homes, all the Booker Prize winning writers and world-class academics would be regulars."

"We've been through all this before. Besides, there must be countless countesses in Cambridge. Haven't you found someone to replace me?"

Albert's voice was soft, barely audible.

"I enjoy living as an expatriate. British sophistication suits me. But I can never replace my Mimi. Of course, you are incomparable, you know that."

"And you are ruining me for other men. They're never as perfect as you."

Margaret had kept secret from Albert something that happened during his last Christmas in Griffith Park. He was preparing for the "great transplantation," as he termed his impending move, and had hired a broker to put his house on the market. Six months had elapsed since her visit to Cambridge. She had assumed the proposal was simply a playful suggestion made during that carefree afternoon exploring the Roman ruins, so it surprised her to find, back in Los Angeles again, that the idea had solidified in his mind, and that he often mentioned it. She protested, but in fact, she was smitten, crazy in love, and ready to succumb.

Albert had decided to give a formal Saturday night Christmas dinner party, a "swan song" for the California phase of his life. The elaborate preparations had taken three weeks. The hostess role reminded her of setting her doll-tables with doll-teacups when she was a little girl. She was aware of being used by him, yet what delightful servitude. She treasured the refined milieu she had always dreamed of. What matter that she was the downstairs maid rather than the maiden in the tower? Two exhausting hours of clean-up followed after the departure of all the guests except Edward, whom Albert characterized as "a well-respected professor, and a dear friend."

It was midnight. Returning into the hallway from the pantry where the cutlery was stored, she glimpsed the raw truth, glossed over for the four years they had known each other, the physicality of Albert's hidden life. The two men stood entwined in the living room. Albert's words were distinct: "Oh, don't worry, I'll get rid of her," and Edward replied with a low moan of urgent physical desire. She froze. The two men disengaged and stepped back a discrete two feet. Pretending that nothing was amiss, she walked into the living room, retrieved her coat from the closet, murmured a polite good-bye, and closed the front door, careful not to slam it.

Once outside, the hysterics began. A private grief, although in public view by the light of the streetlamps, if a neighbor happened to be walking a dog or watching out a window. She stumbled down the hillside to her clunker Datsun. The ancient car squealed and barreled away from the curb. And now screaming and pummeling the steering wheel all the fifteen miles to her tiny apartment in Palms, the wasteland on the fringes of Westwood. A miracle that there was no accident on that dark night. She flung off her ruffled black satin dress, collapsed into bed, and sobbed.

Her sleep was blessedly comatose, and she awoke the next day at noon with a throbbing headache. What would archetypal women do? Ophelia would find a convenient nearby stream in which to drown. But the dry concrete bed of the LA River would hardly suffice. The Hebrew heroine Judith would saw off the heads of both men and impale them on poles outside the gay bar Rage on Santa Monica Boulevard. But the boys inside would probably point and laugh, thinking the heads were campy Halloween masks. What was a sensible modern woman to do? She downed two ibuprofens, and stayed in bed brooding, getting up twice to brew chamomile tea. In the afternoon the telephone rang. It was Albert, thanking her for her help with the party. She told him, in singsong: "I can't see you any-more, it's over, don't call me." And, his puzzlement genu-ine, she knew, "Why, whatever is amiss with my Mimi?"

An excellent question, for which she couldn't find the words to answer. It had taken her until May to allow him back, a cautious distance between them, coffee at a neutral meeting place, a quiet bistro near his home, which was now in escrow. They began a tentative rapprochement, attend-ing a few concerts together, though Albert by this time was in the final throes of all his complicated moving arrange-ments, and had little time to socialize. In early August, the weekend before his departure for Cambridge, he suggested marriage again. She had not refused outright as she should have, but had listened, and skimming over the agony caused by that kiss with Edward, had begun to fantasize once again about the delight of a married life together in England.

❋

A clatter in the hallway, and a baritone male voice calling. "Albert, are you here?"

"That must be James." Albert rose from his chair and hurried toward the voice. Margaret watched the tall, thin newcomer place a brown leather portfolio on a sofa. The two men embraced. She stood up for the introduction.

"This is my friend Margaret Stine. All the way from Los Angeles, to listen to us play."

"Welcome. Albert has told me wonderful things about you. We love our audience."

James's handshake was firm.

"I'll get out of the way of you two." Margaret picked up the diary, walked over to the solarium, and settled in a chaise longue near where the girl had lain.

James brought a music stand out of a closet. Immediately, the sounds of an intense practice session, the "start here, third page fourth measure from the top," the "let's do that again" the "no, no, this is a little slower," James swaying from the waist as he blew into the embouchure hole of his flute, Albert bracing against the piano bench, sometimes almost raising his body up, as he leaned toward the score, his hands flying over the keyboard, feet pumping the pedals. Every few minutes, the music broke off in a jangle.

"James, it needs to be melancholic right here. The water sprite is calling out her sorrow."

"For crying out loud, pay attention to the tempo. Stop the melodrama, please."

The solarium was warming up in the sunlight. As the two men worked and squabbled, Margaret turned the pages of the diary. The story was heartrending. On what date would Julia die? Only a lucky few of the thousands of tubercular patients seeking a rest cure in these mountains had recovered. And what had been the connection between the diarist and the doomed girl? He sounded like a young and anxious husband.

> *19 July 1888.   An altercation with Harold last night. He insists that my visits to J are ill-advised, and demands that I cease them. Her own family is responsible for her care. But I cannot abandon her—I cannot. We grew up together, in our own secret world, we pledged to cherish one another all our lives. She is so frail, so like the pale goddess of the moon, the marble sylph who reclines on her pedestal out in the garden, near the lake. My dearest inspiration, my Naiad, my peerless friend.*

The diarist was not Julia's husband. What then? She read the rest of the entry.

> *The entire Brotherhood is perturbed. What have*
> *our kind, we happy few, to do with women? Other*
> *than our sacred duties to protect our mothers and*
> *sisters, we have no commerce with the feminine sex.*
> *Are H's words an ultimatum? Or is his message*
> *as yet only a warning? I explained to him—*
> *J's demise is near. My few months of vigilance*
> *at her sickbed are not reasonable grounds for*
> *my exalted and intimate friends to sunder me*
> *from our fellowship. Ah, what a catastrophe if*
> *they should desert me. I could not survive.*

An epiphany. Victorian authors were discrete, but this diarist, writing out his distress on a covert page, was frank enough to be understood plainly.

"Albert, no, no, we're not in sync. What's the matter with you today? Start again at the letter M."

The letter M, for Margaret, for Mimi. And so, in every generation, these identical feelings, this same dilemma. Only in the 1880s there was the urgency of incurable disease, the poignancy of early death. The diarist and his Pre-Raphaelite beloved were young and innocent, their motives untainted by self-interest. By contrast she and Albert crawled at a tortoise pace, both in middle age, their game in play for the better part of a decade. Albert dreamed of her as hostess, protectress, muse. She was to him a possession to display, like a fine statue or a painting. But did she feel only a selfless ardent affection? No. He promised deliverance from her banal life—the boring repetitive work as a librarian at the Culver City library, the inane chit chat of her colleagues, her dilapidated neighborhood and down-at-heel apartment, the blind dates with sports-obsessed men. She valued him for his erudition, for his stellar academic connections, for the way he stage-managed glamour.

She lay back and closed her eyes. What a privilege to listen to these two artists struggle to create glorious music in this enchanted setting.

The Carpaccio Dog

THE RAIN BEGAN in the hours before dawn. By six o'clock the city of Venice was waterlogged. Black night gradually turned to gray morning. Fog shrouded the Byzantine domes of Saint Mark's Basilica and the ogival arches of the Doges' Palace. Waves from the canals slapped at the retaining walls, and the swells spilled over and wetted the cobblestones. At one moment the rain poured forth in torrents, in the next it eased to a gentle patter.

An hour after daybreak, Charlotte Wilde, who lived in a small town in downstate Illinois, plodded along in the Piazza San Marco, splashing through shallow puddles, but sidestepping the deep standing pools of water. A black nylon umbrella wobbled in her grasp from gusts of wind. Her damp brown hair had fluffed into a nebula around her face.

She had checked into the Saturnia Hotel the night before, after a transcontinental limbo of twenty-four hours. Exhausted and restless, and having slept not at all, she arose and set out at first light, with no cappuccino to warm her or pane dolce to fill her belly.

She consulted the *Fodor Companion Guide* cradled in her left hand. A gilt bookmark was clipped to a page in the

To view the painting described in this story, visit https://en.wikipedia.org/wiki/St._Augustine_in_His_Study_(Carpaccio)

chapter titled "The Renaissance Dawn." The author discussed the Saints George and Jerome cycles painted by the artist Carpaccio in the first decade of the sixteenth century. The panels remained in their original setting, mounted on the walls of a salon in the Scuola di San Giorgio degli Schiavoni. Professor George Koppel had etched these masterworks in her psyche, could it already be a quarter century ago? He had shown slides of the paintings during a required core curriculum art history course. Her young self, that bewildered college freshman, had hunkered down in the rear of an enormous tiered lecture hall, an anonymous face in a crowd of two hundred students. How like a god was this handsome cocksure professor, flourishing his hands to emphasize his points. Only imagine, the genius Carpaccio, lost in plain sight until Ruskin described the paintings in 1884. In a deep-toned, reverberating voice, the professor recounted the artist's depictions of the noisy pageantry of Venetian regattas. His voice then dropped to a whisper, as if in the hushed corridors of the Marciana library. The master painter had also captured the opulence of tranquil Renaissance reading rooms.

Since that faraway time, Charlotte had ached to see this fabled city. The years had been filled with the responsibility of tending to her ill and aging parents. Her father had died six years ago, and then her mother had suffered a fatal stroke last April. A modest inheritance afforded her the opportunity to travel. What splendid luck to visit in late October, well after the throngs of summer tourists had departed.

How far was the scuola with its treasured Carpaccios? According to the *Fodor*, the distance was short. She set out on the recommended path, along the Grand Canal, up and over several bridges, and then leftward.

Alas, the thread of the directions soon became tangled.

The hotel map folded in her canvas tote bag was of no use. The sinuous curves of the Grand Canal were clear enough, but the rest of the city was a Rorschach blot of pink spaces and black squiggles. In the convoluted logic of these islands the streets were never straight, but twisted and turned and crissed and crossed. They narrowed into alleyways opening into the irregular public squares called campos, once green fields, but for many centuries paved over. Four or more of these alleys branched off from every campo. At odd junctures, little bridges materialized. She trudged up the bridges and then down, turning right, then left, in the general direction of the scuola. No other living soul passed her.

All was silent, save for rain thrumming on the umbrella and plashing off the cobblestones. Water cascaded from the brick facings of houses and from the marble arches of churches. Through the mist glowed the yellows and ochres and rosy pinks of four-story facades, punctuated by dark green shutters. High above, red geraniums dotted the gray stone balconies. A strong odor of finny, dankly fetid marsh-water penetrated even through the fresh scent of rain.

Affixed to many doors were bronze door knockers, heads of the St. Mark lion, scowling exactly at eye level. Graffiti was scrawled next to one of these knockers. Was there crime in this district of the city? Shivering, she pulled her scarf around her neck and mouth. Her raincoat lay plastered to her arms, and was soaked through to the wool lining. Her flannel shirt was damp, and her blue jeans were sodden. Her teeth chattered, and her hands felt numb. As she walked out of an alley and into a campo, she slid on the slick uneven stone pavement. Her body went flying feet first. Landing flat on her back, she lay sprawled, help-less, the ribs of her umbrella broken, the pages of the *Fodor* soused, her tote bag seeping water.

The storm intensified. Water pounded on her face and drenched her clothes. She tried to get up, but a searing pain shot up her right leg, and she found that she could not move. She shut her eyes, and began to sob. Perhaps bitter cold would set in. She might pass out. Many hours would go by before someone discovered her lying unconscious. She could die of pneumonia in a hospital somewhere, at the mercy of strangers who spoke no English, where a stash of fifty euros tucked in her money belt would buy only a few days' supply of amoxicillin.

The rain slowed. Soon it was only a sprinkle, a gossamer mist. Muffled campanile bells tolled. And now, as if in a dream, a wet tongue licked her face. She opened her eyes. A small white dog with a chest of off-white fluff nuzzled her with his black nose. He woofed, and tugged at her coat with his teeth. Why did he seem so familiar? Where had she seen him before? She could not think where.

To her astonishment, her body felt healed. She jumped up without effort. The mutt circled around her. He barked, and ran off down an alley. She thought she heard a soft male voice crooning, "Bellissima Carlotta, this way, and you will be safe. Come out of the wet cold, and into the dry warmth."

She followed the dog. He trotted along a fondamenta parallel to a tiny canal, and turned left. He bounded over a bridge, and sat wagging his tail just outside the titanic bronze door of a gray stone Renaissance building. "Okay, pup, I'm coming," she said aloud, and after clambering across the bridge, she halted in front of the door. A yellow plaque identified the building. *Carpaccio. Orario 10–16. Chiuso il lunedi.* How silly of her not to realize that the scuola was closed to the public this early in the morning. What day was it, could it be Monday, and closed all day? She had left her home at midday on Saturday, and yes, counting on her fingers, it must indeed be Monday. Any visit must wait until tomorrow.

But now, the dog scratched on the door. "It's locked, dear sweet little pup," she said, reaching down and petting him. "See, it won't open." She pushed against the bronze to demonstrate. To her surprise, the door sprang open on well-oiled hinges. The dog padded just inside, paused, and shook the whole of his body, from nose to tail, his fur spewing water drops that glanced on the parquet floor. He bolted pell-mell into the interior and disappeared.

Charlotte hesitated. To enter must be against myriad rules and regulations. Of course any punishment meted out by modern carabinieri must be more farcical than frightening. The dungeons of the Doges' Palace were simply a stage prop for the titillation of tourists. And after all, she should chase after the dog and bring him back outside. She walked into the gloomy room, leaving the door ajar. A calm feeling flooded over her. Her muscles felt as relaxed as after a long soak in the warm mineral spring of a desert spa. Her coat and jeans no longer felt clammy and cold against her skin.

All was quiet. The air was gelid and stale. She peered into the dark, searching for the dog. No sign of him. Suddenly, the bulbs of immense floor lamps clicked, illuminating the entire room. Startled, she looked around. Who had turned on the lights? There was no sign of a caretaker. The system must be automatic. Now, she noticed, the front door was shut. The hinges must be self-closing. Still no dog. Where could he be? There were no openings except for two doors at the far end, which were fastened tight. He must be somewhere inside this room.

But she forgot about the dog as her eyes adjusted and focused. On the walls flashed the bright colors of breathing and pulsing painted figures, set within vistas infused with the opalescent light of Venice, the sun shimmering through the clouds of the lagoon. Smiling, she recognized the pictures. To her immediate left a youthful golden-haired St. George crowed over the bloody carcass of a dragon snarling even after death. Where was her favorite, the scene of that moment in sacred time when a divine voice announces to St. Augustine that his mentor St. Jerome has died? Aha, there it was. She stepped over to study the panel.

The painting depicted the well-appointed studiolo of a humanist Renaissance scholar. Venetian light streamed into the sanctum from a window. Several dozens of vellum books and manuscripts and musical scores lay scattered about. A Ptolemaic armillary sphere, symbol of the new learning, hung suspended from the ceiling. In the foreground near the window, the monk Augustine sat writing at a wood table raised on a dais. In the instant captured by Carpaccio, a voice from the heavens had interrupted the saint. He had turned his head, and gazed toward the window, his quill pen poised in mid-air.

Charlotte glanced at the far left of the composition. In profile a small white dog pointed his black nose toward the window, as if listening also to the divine revelation. Her heart fluttered. Was she perhaps only jet lagged or sleep deprived? Or intoxicated by the dream of Venice, of Serenissima? No, this must be the delirium of a madwoman. For in every detail the image resembled the mutt who had rescued her only a short while ago.

The Miracle of
the Shellflowers

IN THE WILDS of the Sila Massif in Calabria, in the ninth century, near the "toe" of Italy, which in ancient times had been called Magna Graecia, forty monks dwelt in a monastery built on the craggy peak of a steep mountain. There was but one dirt road winding up from the base of the mountain to its crest, a two-hour journey by donkey. The cloisters and refectory abutted a church. Near the building complex a spring of frigid water flowed from a deep cavern.

During the summers a dozen peasants, the youngest a boy of ten and the eldest a graybeard of sixty, left their families who lived in a village on the broad plain below. These simple men tended their sheep and goats in the pastures on the mountainside. When the weather turned cold in October, they drove their flocks back down the mountain.

Every summer Sabbath the shepherds gathered in the church to hear the midday Mass. The monks sat upright on oak benches near the altar. With their hands folded in their laps, they chanted the Psalms *a cappella*, praising God and all His creation in their native Greek tongue. Centuries ago the holy Brother Phantinos, whose moldering bones lay in a crypt under the mosaics of the floor, had translated these poems from the Hebrew of King David. The shepherds stood in a circle in the back of the nave. On their reed pipes they played the Grecian tropes bequeathed from time immemorial to their forefathers, and now to them. The sound of the pipes wove a soprano tapestry over the tenor and baritone voices of the friars. The harmonies spilled into every corner of the church, echoing on the granite stones, sweeping along the aisles of the nave, and, muted by the massive bronze doors, whorling into the courtyard filled with sunlight.

The gentlest of the friars was called Brother Elias. He was learned in the art of distilling plants into medicines. It was said angels whispered the mysteries of healing to him. He slept in a bare stone cell that overlooked the herb garden near the cloisters. The abbot had given him permission to break with the schedule followed by the rest of the monastery. When the bell for Vigils sounded, he arose and meditated alone in his cell. As the roseate dawn lightened, and until midmorning, the garden received his careful tending. Every afternoon from the melting of the snowcap in April to the first blizzards of November, while the other monks copied manuscripts in the scriptorium, he meandered over the entire mountain. He collected specimens of lichen and porcini mushrooms and wildflowers in a large goatskin sack secured at its top with a leather thong. The sun shone bright and fierce, and often toward four o'clock white cumulus clouds piled high on the horizon, sometimes darkening to gray and showering the meadows with balmy rains.

On the day of the summer solstice, Brother Elias hiked to the far side of the mountain, to an outcrop of dolomite boulders. All was quiet, save for the buzz of bumblebees and the hollow tapping of woodpeckers. A slight breeze stirred the curling leaves of the gnarled oaks and rustled the needles of the sentry pines. The sun blazed at the fortieth degree, at three o'clock, the hour of the death of the Christos. As was his custom, the friar bowed his head and murmured the Lord's Prayer. At the final "amen" he opened his eyes, and noticed a mass of bushes growing out of cracks in the boulders. He walked closer to examine them.

Mauve flowers with tracings of delicate blood red spider veins bloomed on the tips of waxy evergreen leaves. The blossoms were the size of almonds and spiraled counterclockwise. They resembled the shape and color of a certain type of shell in the monastery's conchological collection, assembled from rare specimens brought by pilgrims from faraway lands and seas. A black ewe was munching contentedly on these flowers. When she saw the monk, she paused a moment to baah, and then returned to her grazing.

A shepherd's pipe sounded in the air. Soon a youth of fifteen summers who was called Arsenius appeared from behind a ridge. His black hair curled to his shoulders. Goatskins covered him from his shoulders to his knees. His calloused toes stuck out of his leather sandals, the frayed bindings dark from moisture. By his side trotted a white Maremma sheep dog named Sibari.

"Ah, there you are, Zoe, you silly sheep, you are forever straying from your sisters."

He whistled, and Sibari barked and chased Zoe, who bleated as she scrambled down the rocks, the dog nipping at her heels and herding her back to the flock.

Brother Elias greeted Arsenius.

"Young man, do you know this plant?"

"Good friar, I do know it. Every midsummer these evergreens bloom but for one hour, and then the flowers fall and turn to pink dust."

The monk thought a moment. He recalled that he had seen commentary on this shrub in a Greek translation of the Natural History of Pliny the Elder. Moreover, Brother Alexios the librarian had shown him a translated codex authored by the Coptic Desert Father Sabbas that contained a formulary for a healing elixir concocted from the flowers. Sadly, the vellum pages were torn and the description broke off in the middle.

"Ah, I have read of this plant, but have never encountered it. The blooms appear just before three o'clock, the hour of the death of our Lord. It is written that for every blossom a saint is gathered into the heavens, and the angels leave the dust behind."

"If only I could learn the letters. Then I too could read. I would know the wisdom of our Lord."

"My good youth, you already have learned more from simple observation than many scholars ever learn from their reading."

"Alas, my elders despair of me. For I often wander off, and neglect the sheep."

"And what do you do when you wander?"

"I watch the flight of the hawk and smell the fragrance of the pines."

Brother Elias smiled. This boy spoke in poetic rhythms so similar to his own. He thought back thirty years. At this young man's age, Elias had met an anchorite, a holy man who changed his life. Elias was the scion of a merchant family in the Byzantine port of Rhegium. His father and uncles traded in silks and spices. He had learned his letters early from a secular philosopher Leontios, who tutored the boys of wealthy families. Elias committed to memory the sagas of Homer. On the Sabbath, he attended Mass in the cathedral with all his relatives. But as a peach-fuzzed man-boy of fifteen, he fell into a habit of carousing with six boon companions. Several nights a week, the drunken gang staggered through the narrow alleys that radiated out from the quay. They swore oaths in loud voices. Black rats as large as martens scurried over the wharves slick with green algae. The youths unsheathed their swords and sliced these creatures in two, laughing as the blood spurted from the writhing carcasses. Early one morning, just at dawn, dazed from a night of revelry, Elias slumped against a porphyry column in the courtyard of his father's warehouse. The golden-red rays of the rising sun slanted through a door facing the wharf. A figure loomed in the doorway. Through bleary eyes Elias saw the brown robes cinctured with a leather belt, the weathered face, and the straggly gray beard of the hermit Nikolaos, who wandered occasionally through the town. Brother Nikolaos stared at Elias and pointed a scrawny finger.

"Repent, repent. Even Noah in his drunkenness feared the Lord."

And Elias, who in the last few years had mocked all religion, all prayers, scoffing that such fancies were for old women and weaklings, noticed the rosy light of the sun. As if he were sleepwalking, he followed the old monk toward the east, to the caves of the hermits just beyond the city walls. For five years Brother Nikolaos taught Elias to fast and pray. As he lay dying, the aged eremite blessed his young protégé and said:

"Go, seek out the holy mountain, where the Lord, Blessed Be He, has breathed His healing into the plants that flourish there. Study the flora, my son, and the Lord will vouchsafe miracles and wonders."

Brother Elias looked again at the shellflower bushes. Already the blooms were falling, at first one or two fluttering in the air like butterflies on a calm August afternoon, and soon many, swirling like wet snowflakes in a March breeze.

"Young man, could you help me harvest these flowers?"

"Blessed friar, you do me great honor."

The monk and the boy gathered enough blossoms to fill the goatskin sack. Brother Elias threw the sack over his shoulders.

"My dear lad, how are you called?"

"They call me Arsenius."

"Ah, Arsenius. You are a good youth. My name is Brother Elias. Come visit me in the monastery in mid-morning. Always I am in the herb garden."

"I humbly thank you."

Arsenius took up his pipe. He blew a lilting tune, imitating the trill of a lark as it greets the morning sun. He stepped over the ridge back to his flock. Brother Elias set off in the opposite direction on a path toward the monastery. Pine needles and tree nuts and crumbly brown leaves crunched under his feet as he walked, and a hawk rode the wind high overhead. To what good end could he use these shellflowers? He prayed for guidance. Of course he would research all the manuscripts in the library. The librarian Brother Alexios would assist him. God would reveal the mystery, mayhap in a codex, or by other transcendent means.

Brother Elias entered his cell. He laid a sheepskin parchment on the ground and set his sack on top of it. Odd that the goatskin had flattened. He pulled the leather thong apart and peeked inside. No flowers remained, but only three handfuls of pink dust that smelled both sweet and pungent, as if lavender and bergamot orange blossoms mingled with the musk of truffles.

That night, the midsummer night, as Brother Elias slept in his hair shirt on his stone bed, a brittle full moon cast a blinding white light through the narrow aperture high on the wall. An angel appeared in the shape of a youth wearing a mauve tunic. The angel sang:

> *Brew a potion from pink dust of shell flow'r.*
> *See the formula in black letters writ.*
> *God will work wonders in the dark hour,*
> *When bodies lie jumbled and necks lie slit.*

When the monk awakened the next morning, he knew he had dreamt of the shellflowers, but could not remember the details. He glanced at the parchment. A formulary was written on its surface in minuscule Greek script. Ah, an angel must have inscribed the parchment during the night. The friar was not surprised. He often had visions and was accustomed to the esoteric ways of the Divine. God had chiseled the commandments in paleo-Hebrew on the tablets of Moses, and dictated the Gospels to the evangelists in Hellenistic Koine. Now, in the present day vernacular, He communicated formulas for healing medicaments to his faithful servant.

That afternoon, Elias retired to his laboratory. He spread the parchment on his oak workbench and pored over the formulary:

> Crush three handfuls of pink shellflower dust with four thimblefuls of woolen hairs from a black ewe yearling. Dissolve in two small earthenware jars of spring water drawn from the cloister well. Distill over fire until the liquid has reduced in half to a pink elixir. Store in glass bottles in a cool and solitary place.

He kept on hand black ewe yearling wool in an apothecary jar because it was the leaven in many of his remedies. Black sheep were beloved of the Lord, so energetic, so curious, so brave. With his marble mortar and pestle he ground together the pink dust and the black wool. He walked out to the cloister and drew water from the central well into a large wood bucket. The well tapped into the cavern spring, and Brother Elias knew from long experience that the water had curative properties.

In the laboratory he emptied the water into an iron cauldron set on a high trivet on the hearthstone, and stirred in the two ingredients. He kindled a fire under the cauldron, and brewed the mixture for an hour. After the pink liquid had cooled, he decanted it into two glass bottles. He stoppered the bottles with cork and stored them on the top shelf of his oak chest.

To what use could he turn the elixir? He knew not what powers it might have. He could not recall anything more of his dream, though he had faith that in the proper season the Lord would guide him.

A few days later, Arsenius began to visit Brother Elias, at first three times in a week, but then every morning. The youth left Sibari behind to guard the sheep.

"Now be a good dog. This is our secret. The others must not know. I will return in a few hours."

The dog would woof and lie down in the grass, while the flock of three dozen sheep grazed. Just as the bell rang for Lauds, Arsenius appeared in the herb garden. The monk leaned on his spade. He wore a straw hat and wool gloves. Arsenius pulled weeds and watered, plucked off dead leaves and collected seeds, spread sheep and goat manure, and performed any other task that Brother Elias needed. The monk spoke to him, teaching him, guiding him. Brother Elias could see that the boy was growing, even as the plants in the garden grew from thumb-sized seedlings to luxuriant bushes. He sensed that the boy might be attracted to the sacred calling of the monastic life.

All that summer, during the long evenings after the communal supper, Brother Elias walked over to the scriptorium. Brother Alexios brought him every manuscript to examine, at least a chiliad, though many were uncatalogued. He found only the two references he had recollected, that of Pliny and of Sabbas. The glass bottles filled with the pink elixir remained on the shelf.

These years were the time of the Saracen dangers, celebrated in the lore of that countryside. The forces of the

Mohammedans swept north from Arabia across the seas, enlarging their territories and subjugating the populace in the name of Allah.

In September, just before the equinox, the Saracens encamped some four hundred kilometers to the south. The Caliph sent ahead scouts to reconnoiter the countryside. At dawn, four Saracens galloped up the mountain road on their chestnut mares. Halfway up the mountain, in a grassy meadow, ten shepherds slumbered around the embers of a campfire. Their dogs guarded the sheep and goats that were dozing nearby. The horsemen caught sight of the shepherds and surrounded them. The shepherds awoke and jumped up, looking to right and left for escape. They were cornered. The soldiers blindfolded the shepherds, lined them up in a row, and kicked them in the shins from behind. The prisoners thudded to their knees. One of the warriors, who seemed to be the leader, went down the line of captives. While the other three men shrieked an ululating battle cry, he slit each of the shepherds' throats and sawed off their heads with a bronze knife. Bright red blood soaked the ground. The dogs howled and dashed pell-mell around the perimeter of the meadow. The flocks milled about, and then, sensing a world gone mad, they stampeded in all directions. The soldiers pointed at the melee and guffawed among themselves.

It so happened that Arsenius had lain down with his comrades near the fire the previous evening. He slept very little, waking often with a sense of foreboding. He had risen shortly before daybreak, and with Sibari at his heels walked some two hundred meters up the mountain to sit on a favorite boulder and watch the sunrise. He had much to ponder. Brother Elias had taught him to read several of the letters of the alphabet, the alpha and the omega and the gamma. He now knew the formulas for a score of herbal potions. He desired, with all of the force of his slender body and his agile mind, to don the robes of a friar, to follow Brother Elias. His elders said that God had predestined him, like all boys born in his village, to herd sheep. Still, he felt the finger of God tugging at his heart.

He heard the clattering of horses' hooves. Peering down over the meadow, he watched the butchery unfold. He could not move his limbs and his face turned ashen. Sibari whined but never barked.

The soldiers remounted their steeds and urged them even further up the road, to within thirty meters of the lad and his dog. Arsenius could hear the snorting of the horses and the clinking of metal. He fainted and lay inert on the rock shelf of the crag. Sibari nudged the youth's arm with his wet nose, and whimpered.

The horsemen conferred together. They saw no further signs of life. A dense rosy fog blanketed the crest of the mountain. They turned their horses around and spurred them back down the road.

The angelic hosts of the firmament, seeing the slaughter, dispatched two messengers to earth. One angel appeared to Arsenius as he lay unconscious on the rock. The angel sang:

> *Arise! Make thy way to the blessed monk.*
> *Find the elixir from shellflow'rs distilled.*
> *Race to the field littered with heads and trunks.*
> *Our Lord will heal the carnage on the hill.*

Simultaneously a second angel appeared to Brother Elias as he lay sleeping in his cell. The angel sang:

> *Go hotfoot and fetch the shell flow'r balm.*
> *Fly posthaste to the field of shepherds slain.*
> *Then chant in joyous tones King David's Psalms.*
> *Sprinkle the brew. The dead will rise again.*

Arsenius opened his eyes to find Sibari hovering over him. He smelled the doggy breath, and felt the wet tongue licking his face. He patted the dog's head. He dared not look directly at the meadow. What had he dreamt, something about Brother Elias, about the shellflowers, but what exactly? He could not recollect. But he knew he must go to the friar. He scanned the horizon. No horses, no armed men, as far as he could see. He leapt up, and sprinted up the steep road to the monk's cell, the dog bounding alongside.

Brother Elias startled awake. He had dreamt again, something about his elixir, ah, daily he had asked God to reveal its healing qualities, and he dreamt often about it. He removed his hair shirt and laid it on the pallet. He pulled on his brown woolen robe that hung on a peg on the wall. As was his daily habit, he knelt to pray, crossing himself and murmuring over and over, "Lord Jesus Christ have mercy on me a sinner." He fell into his usual meditative trance. But something different happened this morning. After a time, he wasn't sure how long, a commotion interrupted his reverie. Disoriented at first, he finally located the source of the noise, the thuds of a fist pounding on the oak door, and a boy's voice yelling just outside.

"Holy friar, open up. They're dead, they're dead."

The monk pulled open the heavy, creaking door. Outside stood the youth, wet with perspiration and gasping for air, and beside him his panting dog.

"Blessings to you, child, come in, welcome."

As the boy and his dog crossed the threshold, the monk embraced Arsenius, and squatted to shake Sibari's paw.

"What is it, my son?"

"Good friar, listen to me. They came and killed my friends, they're dead, they're dead."

"Sit down. Close your eyes, breathe deeply, be quiet,

and pray for a moment. Then talk, but say each word slowly. Tell me exactly what happened."

The two sat on the stone floor facing each other. The youth spilled out the story of the massacre, in fits and starts, in a torrent of staccato phrases, the monk interjecting "ah's."

Brother Elias closed his eyes and thought back to his dream. An angel had spoken, in sacred rhyme. And now, the words hovered before him, as if engraved on a scroll, black fire on white fire. How could this be? Nowhere did God vouchsafe to mortals the power to raise the dead to life. Yet the angel commanded him to act, and promised this miracle.

"Come with me, my child. We must not lose any more time."

"Where are we going?"

"To the field where your comrades lie fallen."

"To say the blessings for the dead?"

"No. To raise them up. For the Lord, Blessed Be He, has bestowed on us the favor of a potion that can resurrect the dead."

He took an iron key from a peg, and motioned for the youth to join him. They hurried to the laboratory. Sibari padded behind, sniffing the damp grass. The thick mist swirled around them. The youngest monk was just tolling the bell for matins, and the fog muffled its clanging. Woolen robes swished against stone steps as the friars filed into the church.

Brother Elias put the key into the lock of the colossal bronze door of the laboratory, which opened easily on its oiled hinges. He went over to the chest and took down the bottles from the top shelf. He handed one of them to Arsenius.

They trekked carefully down the road, as the incline

was steep, suited to the hooves of sheep and goats rather than the feet of humans. Sibari trotted behind, circling in wide loops as he snuffled in the grasses and scratched at the holes dug by ground squirrels.

After an hour they rounded a bend. Sunlight flooded the meadow. They saw the jumble of bodies and heads, and the red gore oozing and darkening on the ground. They gagged on the stench. Their line of vision bobbed and weaved, as if they stood in the prow of a ship on the Adriatic hurled about by a sirocco cyclone. An instant later, their legs buckled, and they swooned and passed out. The bottles rolled away and came to rest against a hummock. Sibari chased his tail and bayed.

The angels observed the scene from on high, and released a strong scent of lavender, bergamot orange blossoms and musk directly over them. Sibari sniffed the air and then sneezed. The man and the boy coughed, then stretched, and sat up. A gauzy mauve haze shimmered over the meadow. Sibari sat down on his haunches and stayed still, his ears cocked.

The two retrieved the bottles. They walked into the middle of the field among the bodies. They chanted together the poem of the psalmist: "The Lord is my shepherd, nothing shall I want." Brother Elias then took his bottle, uncorked it, and poured a little of the potion into his hand. With a flick of his wrist he sprinkled the liquid over the bodies nearest to him. He repeated this movement, walking around the perimeter of the heap of corpses. Arsenius followed two paces behind him. Over and over they recited: "Blessed be the name of the Lord from this time forth and forever."

When the monk had emptied his bottle, he gave it to Arsenius. The youth then handed the friar the second bottle and the monk sprinkled the elixir over the carcasses until all the liquid was gone. The monk and the boy walked to the edge of the meadow and sat down. After a few moments, lo, the heads were joined back to the trunks, each head to its proper trunk. The blood dried to a fine pink dust that drifted into the air and sparkled in the sunlight.

Brother Elias sat still, a calm smile on his face. How wondrous was the Lord, and how miraculous were His ways. Arsenius sat, his mouth gaping open. He could not believe what he was seeing. He glanced at the monk. Ah, if only he could learn from this man, if he could walk in the way that this friar walked. Sibari came up to him and lay down, nuzzling his wet nose into the folds of his master's goatskin tunic.

Soon the fingers of the bodies twitched and the eyes opened. Indeed, they were living men. They sat up, stretching their arms over their heads. Then they stood, unsteady at first, shifting their feet from side to side and blinking in the sunlight. Their eyes adjusted. Now they were rubbing their necks and looking around, examining each other. They walked over and formed a ragged line in front of the monk and the youth.

Elias and Arsenius stood up. Sibari sat up, occasionally yawning. Brother Elias spoke first.

"Good morrow, my good men."

Now the men jabbered all at once, like chickens that cluck when handfuls of seed are strewn in the dirt of their coop.

"Ho, good morrow, holy friar."

"Those cursed Mohammedans murdered me."

"Yea, they lopped off all our heads."

"My neck itches. Does yours?"

"I do not see a scar on your neck. Is there one on mine?"

"But why are you here, Arsenius? You were not with us when we died."

Brother Elias raised hands, palms facing out, the gesture of blessing.

"Be calm, good souls. Do not clamor, do not worry. You have imagined a horror."

The graybeard spoke. "But we did not imagine it."

A tall muscular fellow chimed in. "Revenge will be ours."

The shepherds shook their fists toward the sky and shouted out, a babel of voices.

"Yea, revenge!"

"Stay out of this. Monks are of no use in times of war."

"Anathema on the Mohammedans."

"May God strike them dead."

"Let their bodies be hacked to pieces!"

"May Satan cast them into the fires of hell!"

Brother Elias spread his arms further apart in the air, palms out in blessing.

"No, my brothers, listen to me. Hearken to the words of the Lord."

He spoke barely above a whisper. They watched him. They dropped their hands and lowered their voices, although they continued to scowl and clench their fists and mutter curses. He looked straight into their eyes, one after the other, holding each man's gaze for a quarter minute. They ceased talking and their arms dangled loose at their sides.

Then the friar spoke slowly, enunciating each consonant and elongating each vowel.

"My beloveds, it was only an illusion, a work of the Evil One, who envies our peaceful mountain. The Evil One casts his Evil Eye out of a jealous rage. He begets fear and hatred among men."

The graybeard swayed slightly, as if spellbound. He mumbled "Yea, the holy monk speaks words of truth."

The friar now raised his arms higher and looked up to the sky. The shepherds with one movement also shifted their eyes heavenward. They wished to see what the monk saw.

"Our gracious Lord, Blessed Be He, has today banished the Evil One. He has restored His peace. Hallelujah. Praise God. Amen."

"Amen," answered the shepherds, in unison, as if they were reciting the Mass. They looked at one another and began to smile.

"Peace be with you," they murmured, and they embraced, and each kissed one another upon the cheeks. Then they strode off, whistling for the dogs to fetch the sheep and goats. All as it should be, a normal autumn day.

Arsenius entered the monastery as a disciple to Brother Elias. Both men grew in wisdom and loving-kindness. The fame of their elixirs spread far and wide, even south to Constantinople and north to the forests of the Franks.

❈

In the fourteenth century an anonymous master painted a fresco cycle that recounted the legend of the two blessed friars. The artist created a backdrop of cobalt blue sky punctuated with yellow stars. In the early scenes, a monk and a boy gathered mauve flowers. Carmine red blood spurted from the stumps of shepherds' necks. In the foreground, a white dog frolicked with many white and a single black sheep. Angels with the rose cheeked faces of young boys hovered in the heavens above. In later episodes, two monks in brown robes walked in a landscape dotted with cypresses and Roman arches. The painter applied shimmering gold leaf to the haloes that surrounded the heads of the monks and the angels.

These frescoes cover the walls and ceiling of a chapel near the apse of a Romanesque church in a monastery on the summit of a mountain in Calabria. The abbey is difficult of access and therefore not included in a typical tourist itinerary. Some stalwart travelers find their way to this remote place, and it is not unusual for a visitor to sit alone in the hush of that chapel, studying the frescoes, and meditating on their meaning.